NEVER TRUST A SNAKE

Driskoll looked at Kellach's neck. A strange red scar was forming there, and the skin around it was red too. "Kellach," he said, panicking. "You've been bitten."

"I'm okay," he said, rubbing his neck. "I felt a sharp pain. But . . ."

"But what?" Moyra asked.

Kellach gazed at her. "Then it was gone. I don't really feel anything right now. But that snake . . . I didn't do any magic to it. How did it just burn up like that?"

Driskoll went to pick up the basket and noticed that Suma wasn't in it.

"Right there," Moyra said, pointing.

The little green snake lay coiled on the ground. Its head was in striking position, and it was glaring at the ashes of the snake.

"It almost looks like Suma attacked the snake," Kellach said slowly.

Driskoll shook his head. "How could an ordinary little garden snake do something like that?"

KNIGHTS
OF THE
SILVER
DRAGON
SD

MARK OF THE YUAN-TI

KERRY DANIEL ROBERTS

KNIGHTS
OF THE
SILVER
DRAGON

BOOK 12

COVER & INTERIOR ART
EMILY FIEGENSCHUH

MIRROR
STONE

Mark of the Yuan-ti
©2006 Wizards of the Coast, Inc.

Published by Wizards of the Coast, Inc. KNIGHTS OF THE SILVER DRAGON, MIRRORSTONE, and their respective logos are trademarks of Wizards of the Coast, Inc., in the U.S.A. and other countries.

All Wizards of the Coast characters, character names, and the distinctive likenesses thereof are property of Wizards of the Coast, Inc.

Printed in the U.S.A.

Cover and interior art by Emily Fiegenschuh
Cartography by Dennis Kauth

First Printing: April 2006
Library of Congress Catalog Card Number: 2005935560

9 8 7 6 5 4 3 2 1

ISBN-10: 0-7869-4033-6
ISBN-13: 978-0-7869-4033-2
620-95563740-001-EN

U.S., CANADA,
ASIA, PACIFIC, & LATIN AMERICA
Wizards of the Coast, Inc.
P.O. Box 707
Renton, WA 98057-0707
+1-800-324-6496

EUROPEAN HEADQUARTERS
Hasbro UK Ltd
Caswell Way
Newport, Gwent NP9 0YH
GREAT BRITAIN
Please keep this address for your records

Visit our web site at www.mirrorstonebooks.com

For Boots,
who's watching it all
from a cloud somewhere.

CURSTON

1. Cathedral
2. The Westgate
3. The Oldgate
4. Driskoll and Kellach's home
5. Moyra's home
6. Zendric's tower
7. The Skinned Cat
8. Watchers' Hall
9. Selik's dungeon
10. Blacksmith's shop

CHAPTER

1

"Please?" Driskoll asked.

"No." Driskoll's father, Torin, rifled through the piles of scrolls littering his desk without looking up.

"But why not?" Driskoll asked.

Nearby, a barrel-chested dwarf with a salt-and-pepper beard stood at the office door, leaning his double-edged axe against the doorframe. "Sir, we must leave now," he said in an agitated voice.

Torin glanced up. "Right, Gwinton," he said. "I'll be there in a minute."

Driskoll didn't back down. "I can take care of it myself," he pleaded. "I'll feed it and groom it and take it for walks and everything."

"Just drop it," Kellach whispered in his younger brother's ear. "Now's not the time to be asking him."

Driskoll glared at Kellach.

Torin continued sifting through scrolls as if Driskoll and

Kellach weren't there. "Blast," he swore. "This office is a mess."

"Sir," Gwinton insisted. "The blacksmith . . . We really must go."

"We're not going anywhere until I find that search warrant," Torin growled, tossing an armful of scrolls to the floor.

"But the blacksmith—he may be infected too," Gwinton said.

Torin yanked at a desk drawer. "We can never be too careful—aha!" He pulled out a torn and moldy-looking scroll. "Let's go."

Gwinton held the door open wide as Torin slipped the scroll into his pocket, straightened his captain's uniform, and strode toward him.

Driskoll watched as his father placed his powerful arm on Gwinton's hunched shoulder. "Now I want you and all the other watchers to be on your guard," Torin said in a low voice. Gwinton nodded obediently and Driskoll could see the excitement in both men's eyes as they prepared to venture out on another important job guarding the city.

"But, Dad, what about my pet?" Driskoll called after his father. "I'm responsible enough to get one."

Torin stopped and glanced at Driskoll. "Look," he said. He was still frowning, but slightly less than before. "Show me how responsible you are. You can start by cleaning up my office. Then maybe we'll talk about it."

He swept out the door and slammed it behind him, locking it out of old habit.

"Yes!" Driskoll grinned at Kellach. "What do you think I should get? A hedgehog, maybe? How about a bat? I'd love to have a pet bat. It could fly around and bring me bugs."

Kellach shuddered. "Yeah, well, before you get too animal crazy, just remember what Dad said. You have to clean this office."

"Uh huh," Driskoll said. "So I just tidy it up and I'm done."

Kellach gestured at the piles of parchment on the floor around Torin's desk. "Have you looked at this place lately? It hasn't been cleaned in a dragon's age."

"Yeah, but you'll help me, right?" Driskoll asked. "I mean, you could, you know . . . "

"Do a little magic?" Kellach strolled behind Torin's desk and sat down. "Sorry. This is your job, little brother. And by the way, the floor is filthy." He picked up a scroll and scanned it the way he'd seen Torin do.

"Come on, Kellach," Driskoll begged. "This will take me all day."

"Exactly," Kellach replied, putting his worn leather boots up on his father's desk. "And Dad will be back soon, so you should probably shake a unicorn's tail and get on with it." He returned to the scroll he probably shouldn't have been reading.

Driskoll sighed. Kellach was right. This was his job. "Maybe I could get a falcon," he muttered as he retrieved some scrolls from the floor. "I've heard you can train them to fetch on command."

He spotted an old barrel in a corner and started stuffing everything he found on the floor inside it. After fifteen minutes, the barrel was full of broken quill pens, rotten apple cores, some large dead spiders, a smelly boot, and various crumpled scrolls Driskoll hoped weren't too important.

"There," he sighed, wiping his hands on his patched jacket and looking around. "The floor is clean. Sort of."

Kellach didn't look up. "Walls," he said.

Driskoll glanced around the office. The walls were so covered in grime Driskoll had no idea what color they actually were. One wall was lined with some very old and very dirty animal-head trophies. Dusty black cobwebs hung from the ears of two red-eyed yeth hounds, and a minotaur was missing one of its horns. Then there was a pair of wild boars that looked like they'd been attacked by a swarm of giant moths.

"Yuck." Driskoll curled his lip at the sight. "Come on, Kellach. Give me a hand here."

"It's your job," Kellach repeated.

Driskoll put his hand on his sword and thought for a moment. His sword always seemed to give him the strength he needed. "You're right," he said finally. "And I wouldn't ask, but you're so *good* at magic. I even heard Zendric tell Dad that he was starting to feel like the apprentice wizard and that you were the master."

"Really?" Kellach looked up. "Did Zendric really say that?"

Driskoll shrugged. "Well, something like that. But you really are getting a lot better. He said those spells just glide off of you."

"They glide off of me, huh?" Kellach said.

Uh oh. Driskoll realized he'd gone too far. Sometimes, trying to flatter Kellach backfired on him when Kellach realized what he was up to. "Well, what I meant was . . ."

Driskoll trailed off. Kellach had already closed his eyes and had begun to chant.

4

Driskoll's heart beat hard. This might still be okay. Maybe Kellach hadn't realized that Driskoll was making everything up about Zendric and the spells. And maybe Kellach would perform a flying spell so Driskoll could fly around the room while he cleaned. Or maybe he could conjure up a shining charm so that everything Driskoll touched became dazzlingly clean.

Driskoll shivered. That was strange—Kellach's magic had never had that effect on him before. Then without warning his legs fell out from under him and he slid onto the floor.

"Ha!" Kellach jumped from the chair. "It worked."

Driskoll looked around. The grimy wooden floorboards were gone. In their place was a white, slippery sheet of something that felt very cold.

"Kellach! What did you do? How is this supposed to help me?"

"It's an ice spell," Kellach chuckled. "It just glided right off of me. Ha ha." He skated out from behind the desk. "Come on, it'll be fun," he continued. "And I'll help."

Finally able to stand, Driskoll tried to dodge Kellach, but he lost his balance and fell into him. They toppled to the frozen floor.

"By Saint Cuthbert, your head is harder than the ice," Kellach laughed, rubbing his shoulder.

Driskoll wobbled back to his feet and faced his older brother. "Kellach, this isn't what I had in mind. Dad will kill us."

Out of the corner of his eye, Driskoll saw a figure in the open doorway. His stomach sank as he realized only one person could unlock that door. He wondered why his father wasn't yelling yet.

But then he spotted a blaze of red hair.

"Your dad really should get better locks," Moyra yawned, dropping her lock pick in her shoulder bag and tossing her red hair back. "And where have you two been? You were supposed to meet me out front a whole—" She looked at the floor and stopped. "Holy harpies, is that ice?"

Moyra was the boys' best friend and the only other Knight of the Silver Dragon in Curston besides Zendric. She took a step inside and glided across the room, neatly stopping herself by clutching the barrel with her fingertips. "This is fantastic, Kellach."

"Thank you." Kellach bowed. "Come on, let's have a race." Moyra joined him, and they slid along the ice toward the far window.

"No!" Driskoll shouted. "I'm supposed to be cleaning."

"You wanted me to help you," Kellach called over his shoulder. "And I am. Watch." He held the wide sleeve of his faded purple cloak up to the wall and skated alongside it, leaving a brownish, streaky mark on the wall.

"See? Perfectly clean." Kellach shook the dirt out of his sleeve.

"I don't know, Kellach," Moyra said, sliding over to the wall. "That's just a big ugly mark. I don't think your dad will like that."

Driskoll dropped his face into his hands. "Please make the ice go away, Kellach."

"Oh come on," Kellach said. "It's more fun this way."

Driskoll looked up. Kellach was making a bigger mess, skating all along the wall and creating more giant streaks. He

6

stopped at the trophy wall. "This place will be so clean, you'll be getting a pet sooner than you think," Kellach said, looking up at the mangy-looking animal heads. "Hey, maybe Dad'll get you one of these." He pointed at the wild boars and glanced over his shoulder at Driskoll. "You know, they say pets start to look like their masters after awhile," Kellach grinned. "But this one already looks a lot like you!"

Driskoll forgot that he was supposed to be cleaning. He held his hands up to his mouth, pointing his fingers out at Kellach so that he resembled a wild boar getting ready to charge. He slid toward Kellach just as the doorknob began to turn.

Driskoll didn't notice. He collided with Kellach, knocking him into the wall. They sat in a dazed pile on the floor.

Something rattled above the boys. Driskoll looked up just in time to see the boar's head coming loose from its hanger. The big hairy trophy slid down toward Driskoll, making a heavy scratching noise along the wall. Driskoll was still too dazed to move.

Just as Driskoll realized he had better get out of the way, the trophy flew outward. It was suspended in the air like an ugly hairy ghost for a moment, and then fell to the ice with a cracking thud.

Driskoll looked at Kellach, whose arms were raised in a spell.

"Thanks," Driskoll breathed.

But Kellach had turned to the door, and his smug smile turned to a grimace.

Driskoll turned too. He followed the long gash the trophy had made as it skidded along the ice. It led directly to the now open office door. The boar head stared at them from beneath the foot of the last person in the world Driskoll wanted to see right now: his father.

CHAPTER

2

Driskoll wasn't sure who looked angrier, Torin or the wild boar head caught under his father's foot.

Out of the corner of his eye, Driskoll saw Kellach wave his arms. The ice melted instantly, leaving puddles of water here and there on the wooden planks.

"What were you thinking?" Torin bellowed. "Ice! In my office! What if I'd brought someone important with me, or a prisoner?"

"We were just trying to make the work easier," Kellach muttered.

Driskoll cringed at his brother's answer. Hadn't Kellach learned by now that you had a much better chance of escaping unharmed if you kept quiet when Torin was this angry?

"Easier?" Torin's thundering voice bounced against the walls and echoed back in Driskoll's chest. He was sure everyone in Watchers' Hall could hear. "You don't turn my office into a playground."

Gwinton came up behind Torin. "Everything all right, sir? Is there anything I can do?"

"Yes." Torin flipped around. "Please escort these three to the prison."

Driskoll looked at Torin. He couldn't be serious.

"I beg your pardon, sir?" the old watcher asked, his watery eyes bulging.

"You heard me—to jail. These three have vandalized an office of the watch."

Gwinton looked at Driskoll and back at Torin. "Sir, you've been working many long hours. I know you are tired and angry but—"

Gwinton nodded at Driskoll, who quickly put an innocent look on his face.

Torin sighed angrily. "Fine. Just get them out of here. I'll deal with them later."

"I guess this means I won't be getting a pet," Driskoll muttered as Gwinton herded the kids out the door and closed it gently behind them.

"What did you three do now?" he asked as they followed him down the hallway.

"We would have been fine if Driskoll hadn't been messing around," Kellach groaned.

"Me? I'm not the one who turned Dad's office into an ice pond."

Moyra snickered.

"An ice pond?" Gwinton stopped and faced them. He shook his head. "Look, you three. Torin's got enough on his mind over this disease that's spreading around town. Take my advice and stop getting into trouble, or next time he really will throw you in prison. And he'll toss the key into the ruins."

Kellach stopped walking. "Disease? Since when do the watchers worry about a disease? Isn't that a job for the clerics?"

Gwinton scratched his neck. "It's a job for us when no one else can do it." He looked around and lowered his voice. "All the clerics were struck last night. Every single one of them. They're all laid up in St. Cuthbert's. And now the blacksmith . . . Your father suspects foul play."

"Foul play?" Driskoll piped. "But why would he think—"

"Shhh," Gwinton waved his hands in the air. "It's enough that your father suspects it."

"What kind of disease is it?" Moyra asked.

Gwinton opened his mouth to answer and then shut it. He wagged a finger at them. "I know what you're doing," he said. "And I've already told you too much. The last time you three got involved, all of my watchers got frozen by a bunch of crazed mummies."

"Believe me," Moyra said. "If it's some kind of disease, we won't get involved."

Gwinton scratched his neck again. "Good," he said. "Now go on home before you catch it." He heaved open the gigantic oak doors of Watchers' Hall.

"And stay out of trouble," he called as the kids stumbled into the sunlit street. The doors of Watchers' Hall shut behind them. Driskoll's clothes, which had felt so warm in the chilly office, now felt heavy and hot in the summer sun, and he broke into a sweat.

Kellach headed toward the center of town.

"Well thanks to Kellach, I'll never get a pet," Driskoll grumped as he followed his brother. "We're lucky we didn't get sent to prison."

"Oh goblin droppings," Moyra laughed. "Your dad just lost his temper. You don't really think he'd send his own sons to prison, do you?"

Driskoll squinted at her. "Did you just arrive in Curston or something? That's my dad we're talking about, the captain of the watch. When he's tired, there's no telling how angry he'll get. We'd probably be hanging from our toes right now if Gwinton hadn't come along."

Driskoll called after his brother, who was walking several paces ahead. "Wait up, Kellach! Where are you going? Home is that way!"

"I'm not going home," Kellach snorted. "I want to know why Dad would be investigating a disease." He turned in the direction of the Cathedral of St. Cuthbert.

Moyra stopped. "Oh no," she said. "You two may be my best friends, but I am not following you over there."

"Why not?" Kellach asked. "You heard Gwinton. Dad suspects foul play. And St. Cuthbert's seems to be where it all started."

Driskoll lagged behind for a moment but ran to catch up. "Kellach, aren't we in enough trouble without catching some horrible disease?"

"Oh come on," Kellach said. "We're not going to catch anything. We don't even have to go inside." He looked hard at Driskoll. "And anyway, helping to solve this illness situation would show Dad how responsible you are."

Driskoll's eyes lit up. "Yeah," he said. "And then I could get a pet." He looked at Moyra. "What are we waiting for?"

Moyra shook her head as she followed them. "It must be some kind of brain disease," she muttered. "And you two have the worst case I've ever seen."

■ ▮ ▮ ▮ ▮

Driskoll always thought the Cathedral of St. Cuthbert, with its huge statues of saints and deities said to be carved by giants, its needle-like spires that reached to the sky, and its stained glass windows that glimmered like shooting stars for a few brief seconds every day, looked like something out of another world.

Being in the very center of town, St. Cuthbert's was always a place of bustling activity. But today, it was strangely silent. Huge, blood red sashes draped halfway around the building, but were ripped and torn in some spots, making it look like someone had begun to open a very large gift, but had run away in fright or disgust.

"Quarantine," Kellach muttered.

They all stood staring at the building from a safe distance. "What?" Driskoll and Moyra asked at once.

"The place has been cut off from entry," Kellach explained. "No one's allowed inside."

"And there's a good reason for that," Moyra added as Kellach walked slowly toward the cathedral's steps. "This disease is probably catching."

"But someone's got to help the clerics," Kellach said as he continued walking. "They're the only ones who know how to heal disease."

"So what happens when all the clerics are sick?" Driskoll asked.

"The watchers take care of them, that's what happens," Moyra answered before Kellach had a chance.

They reached the base of the stone steps leading to the great doors. Driskoll pointed at a lone watcher resting at the top. The watcher's head bowed forward on his chest.

Kellach clucked his tongue. "Asleep at his post," he huffed. "Wait until I tell Dad."

Before anyone could stop him, Kellach marched up to the sleeping watcher and tapped him on the shoulder. "Wake up!"

The watcher fell over onto the step. Kellach knelt and put his head to the man's chest. "Still breathing," he announced. "He's just . . . asleep."

Driskoll crept up beside Kellach. "Look," he said, pointing at the main doors, which had been propped open slightly. "The doors are open, and the red sashes across the entry have been torn. Someone's gone inside."

"Good." Moyra turned to leave. "That means someone's taking care of the clerics. Now let's get going."

But Kellach began walking toward the doors.

"No, Kellach," Driskoll said. "Moyra's right. Who knows what we would catch. And this disease could be fatal."

Kellach stopped. "But breaking through quarantine sashes is against the law. And that fellow," Kellach motioned to the sleeping watcher on the stairs, "is too lazy to care. We should at least check to see who broke the quarantine so we can report back to Dad. Don't you want to show him that you're responsible?"

14

Driskoll sighed and turned to Moyra. She glared up at the two of them from the street, her arms folded in front of her. She shook her head.

Driskoll turned toward Kellach.

"Driskoll, no." Moyra called. But Driskoll was thinking about his future pet and followed Kellach through the open door.

"Gargoyle heads," a voice muttered behind him a few seconds later. He turned. Moyra had joined them after all. She held a handkerchief to her mouth, and her voice was muffled. "I have to follow you everywhere to keep you out of trouble."

Driskoll tried his best to grin reassuringly at her, but she wouldn't look at him.

They followed Kellach into the entrance area of the cathedral.

It was a wide, plain room with tiled floors and high windows that looked into the main section of the cathedral. Normally, there would be a cleric or two hurrying by, but the room was completely empty and silent.

Directly in front of them, two arched wooden doors led farther inside. Like the front doors, these were open.

That's odd, Driskoll thought. These doors were always closed when he was there before.

Kellach looked around. "I don't see anything so far," he whispered. He took a few steps forward through the archway, passing into the cavernous main chamber. Driskoll followed.

The Cathedral of St. Cuthbert was designed to draw your eyes upward above the stone arches and pillars, above the hanging incense burners, above the simple stone altar. Your eyes were meant to be dazzled by the jewel-like stained-glass windows with their intricate, geometric patterns. Set high in the stone walls, the windows made Driskoll feel dizzy almost instantly.

Kellach nudged him and put his finger to his lips to indicate silence. He pointed.

There was an open grate about halfway up the aisle, where the clerics warmed themselves in winter and burned their sacrificial incense during the warmer months. Driskoll had heard somewhere that the grate was also a secret passageway that led into the catacombs beneath St. Cuthbert's, and he'd always been interested in checking them out.

But just beyond the grate, near the altar, stood a pack of huge shaggy dogs. Driskoll felt the hair on the back of his neck stand up. He tried to take a step backward, but both of his feet were suddenly rooted to the spot. He looked at Kellach and Moyra. They both looked confused, and they weren't moving either.

Driskoll looked at his feet, but he couldn't find them. They were lost beneath an ocean of crawling, weaving, shimmering bodies. And Driskoll was sure he saw several pairs of yellow eyes looking up at him.

CHAPTER

3

S nakes!" Moyra whispered in a frightened voice that Driskoll almost didn't recognize. It was true. The main aisle of St. Cuthbert's was alive with hundreds of snakes—gray, brown, black—all blending into the mottled colors of the tiled floor. They were moving in the same direction, away from the shaggy animals and toward the doors through which the kids had just entered.

Moyra struggled against the mass of slithering bodies, her face as white as the handkerchief held over her mouth.

"They're not after us," Kellach breathed, standing calmly in the river of moving reptiles. "They seem to be heading out the door."

Kellach looked again at the dogs near the altar, which Driskoll now realized were not just dogs, but wolves all gathered in a circle. Between their spindly legs, Driskoll could make out a long green line stretched across the tiled floor. The creatures stared at the line as if they were about to pounce on it.

But Driskoll still couldn't move—none of them could. The snakes were streaming toward the door so fast that the kids' feet were completely buried.

"Just stand still," Kellach whispered, watching the shaggy creatures up ahead.

Driskoll could hear Moyra breathing hard. He reached out to touch her shoulder to reassure her, but a low guttural growl stopped him.

"Dire wolves," Kellach murmured. "About ten of them."

Someone whispered something. Driskoll looked at Moyra and then at Kellach, but they were both glancing around as if they'd heard it too. Driskoll looked back at the wolves. The green line twitched at their feet, and Driskoll heard the whispering again.

"Help me," the voice said. Driskoll wondered if one of the sick clerics were nearby, but he couldn't see anyone else.

It was at that moment that Driskoll realized the long green line at the creatures' feet was another snake, and he was pretty sure it was dead. So why were the wolves watching it so intently?

One of the wolves turned and sniffed the air. It broke away from the group and focused its red eyes on the three kids. A long trail of saliva dripped from the creature's black-rimmed mouth. Driskoll felt like he was face-to-face with something horribly evil, something that would rip him limb from limb not for food, but for the sheer pleasure of it.

The dire wolf gave a long, ear-piercing howl.

The green snake twitched again, but the dire wolves ignored it now. The leader of the pack took a step toward the kids.

Driskoll was relieved to see that his feet were now free, all the snakes having escaped out the doors of St. Cuthbert's.

"We'll fight them," Moyra whispered faintly.

"No," Kellach said between clenched teeth. "There are too many of them. There's another way out."

The wolves took another step forward.

Driskoll glanced back at the open doors. "Should we run? I think we should run!"

"No," Kellach said. "Wait. I have a plan."

Driskoll couldn't see Kellach's face from where he was standing, but he hoped that Kellach didn't look afraid. "Just don't move," Kellach said.

The wolves broke into a run. Driskoll wasn't aware of anything except burning red eyes, long sharp teeth, and the putrid smell of death. And it was all coming closer.

Kellach raised his arms.

The dire wolves jumped over the grate in the floor. They were only a few feet away now, and Driskoll could hear a thousand voices within their howls—voices of the undead wailing piteously. He felt the wolves' hot breath sear his skin, and the sharp ends of their fur scratched like knives.

There was a flash of light and a wolf lunged at Kellach, who seemed to slip beneath it. A second later, the howling was in Driskoll's ears as another creature jumped toward him. Driskoll lost his balance and slid forward as the wolf flew over him. He heard the wolf land just behind him, and its claws scraped on something.

Driskoll tried to get up, but his feet slipped. He lay across a dazzlingly white and bitterly cold floor. Kellach's ice! Around him, the wolves were stunned momentarily as they slipped and skidded on the slippery surface. They screeched and howled in confused anguish.

The wolves suddenly ignored the kids and tried desperately to get away from the ice. But it was everywhere, all along the tiled floor of the cathedral, up the pillars and columns, along the walls, almost up to the stained-glass windows. It looked like a shimmering winter had set into St. Cuthbert's.

Driskoll couldn't see the green snake anymore. For a confused moment, he wasn't sure what to do.

But someone was lifting him up. It was Kellach. "Now you can run!"

CHAPTER

4

I told you going there was a bad idea!" Moyra yelled as they charged away from the Cathedral of St. Cuthbert.

They ran back toward Watchers' Hall. Gwinton sat alone on the stone steps.

"Gwinton!" Driskoll cried. "Dire wolves! In St. Cuthbert's!"

The old watcher stared blankly at the kids. "What?"

"They won't be there long," Kellach panted. "I did an ice spell and, well, everyone knows dire wolves hate ice."

"I didn't know that," Driskoll said. "I thought you were just, you know, out of ideas."

Kellach straightened his back. "I'm never out of ideas."

Driskoll rolled his eyes. Gwinton still stared blankly at the kids. Driskoll tapped him on the shoulder. "Sergeant Gwinton?"

"What?" he started.

"There's a pack of dire wolves in the Cathedral of St. Cuthbert. We thought you should know."

"St. Cuthbert's? You went to St. Cuthbert's?" Gwinton asked. His voice sounded oddly strained and his eyelids were drooping. No one said anything for a minute, and Gwinton looked away.

"So why are you here again?" the old watcher asked.

"Because," Kellach said patiently. "There is a pack of dire wolves in St. Cuthbert's. They're probably gone by now—maybe somewhere in the city. But we thought the watchers ought to know. Gwinton, are you all right?"

"I'm fine," Gwinton said thickly. "Wolves. Right." He groaned as he stood up. "I'll alert your father."

He didn't move.

The kids stared at him. "Would you like us to tell Dad for you?" Kellach offered.

"No, no," Gwinton said distractedly. "You kids should definitely not bother him right now. I'll tell him." He turned around slowly. "Wolves. Cathedral," he muttered. "Wolves. Cathedral." He went back inside Watchers' Hall, mumbling to himself.

"Do you think he's all right?" Driskoll asked as he watched Gwinton stumble up the steps.

"I'm worried about Moyra too," Kellach said, gesturing toward her.

Driskoll glanced at their friend. She looked as white as the ice. "Er, maybe you—we—should rest," he said.

"What's the matter?" Kellach asked her. "You've fought off wolves before."

Moyra was silent for a moment. "It's—it's not the wolves," she stammered. "It was those snakes. I hate snakes."

She looked around at the bleak gray buildings and tower that made up Watchers' Hall. "A snake bit me this morning," she continued, rubbing the back of her hand. "I was sweeping out the fireplace and it was lying in there. I thought it was dead. I went to move it and the dirty thing bit me."

"By the gods," Kellach swore. "You never mentioned that."

"Yeah." Her voice was still a little shaky. "I-I was trying to forget about it."

Driskoll saw that she was trembling, and her terrified face reminded him of the green snake frozen in fear.

"We should rest here until Gwinton comes back with more watchers," Kellach said, leaning against a railing on the steps. "How in the name of magic did those wolves get into the city? And in broad daylight?"

Driskoll shrugged. "I think they were after that snake."

Kellach rubbed his chin. "That was strange too," he mused. "Where did all those snakes come from? And where were they going?"

"It's obvious they were trying to get away from those dire wolves," Driskoll answered, still watching Moyra carefully. She sat down on the steps and hugged her knees to her chest. She didn't look up at either of them.

"But what were they doing in there?" Kellach repeated.

"Did you notice that all of the snakes were moving away, but there was one left?" Driskoll asked. "It was alone near the wolves. And they were about to attack it—until they saw us."

"I didn't see anything but the dire wolves," Kellach answered sharply.

"That snake was so little," Driskoll said. "All of those other snakes had abandoned it. They left it there all by itself to face the dire wolves."

"Oh please," Kellach said. "That's just what snakes do. Everybody knows you can't trust snakes."

Driskoll remembered the voice he'd heard. "Did you hear someone say something in there?"

"As a matter of fact, I did," Kellach said. "I thought it was a cleric."

"Yeah," Driskoll agreed. "Or maybe that snake was trying to tell us something."

Kellach looked at Driskoll. "That is the most ridiculous thing I have ever heard," he snapped. "It was just a snake. Probably dead by now anyway."

"I don't think so," Driskoll shot back. "I bet it's alive, and it's wondering why all the other snakes abandoned it."

"Well why don't you just go back and check on it, then?" Kellach asked.

"I think I will." Driskoll turned toward St. Cuthbert's.

"Say 'hi' to the dire wolves," Kellach called after him. "I'm sure they'd love to have you for dessert."

❦ ❦ ❦ ❦ ❦

Driskoll hadn't walked more than a block before he heard Kellach following him. "What are you doing here?"

"Keeping you out of trouble, for one thing," Kellach answered. "And for another, Gwinton and Dad never came out. So someone has to check on those wolves."

"What happened to Gwinton and Dad?"

"Most likely Dad's too busy," Kellach answered importantly.

"He probably knows I can handle the wolves since I did the ice spell, so he's leaving them to me."

Driskoll rolled his eyes. Secretly he was glad his brother was tagging along. He noticed that Moyra was silently following too. She still looked shaken and white, but her usual determined look had returned to her face.

At the foot of the cathedral's steps, Driskoll looked up at the spires. He could barely see the top, and he started to feel dizzy again.

"The watcher's still asleep," Kellach said, touching the uniformed man with his toe.

"Kellach, be quiet," Driskoll whispered. "The wolves could still be here, waiting for an ambush."

"Naw," Kellach scoffed "That's a permanent ice spell. They're terrified of ice. And they won't be back here for a while."

"The question is, where did they go?" Moyra asked. "I hate to think of those things roaming the city."

"I don't hear them anywhere," Driskoll said. "Let's just check on the snake. Then we can go deal with those wolves."

Everyone inched slowly toward the main doors, listening carefully for the horrible howling.

Driskoll peeked inside. "Nothing in here," he whispered, scanning the entry area. The others followed as he walked carefully across the frozen floor toward the doors that led into the main chamber. The doors were still open, and he looked inside.

The floor of the cathedral was still covered with ice, and the charred remains of the wolves lay strewn across the floor. They all gasped.

"I thought they ran away," Kellach said.

"But something burned them," Driskoll said. "Did your ice do that?"

Kellach shook his head. "It's ice. How could it burn them?"

Driskoll strained his eyes to see the spot where he'd noticed the snake, but the ice formed a white carpet that covered everything. He took a step inside the chamber.

"Can you make the ice disappear, Kellach?"

Kellach looked around and muttered a chant. The next moment the ice was gone and little puddles were everywhere. The wolves' deathly scent mixed with the smell of burnt fur.

Driskoll held his nose as he stepped over the blackened remains of the wolves. He stepped carefully, avoiding the puddles and trying not to slip. He advanced up the aisle to the spot where he'd seen the snake. Behind him, Kellach bent down and studied the dire wolves.

"My ice didn't do this," he said grimly.

"Then who, or what, did it?" Moyra asked, coming up beside him.

Kellach didn't answer and Driskoll was barely listening. His eyes scanned the damp floor for the little snake.

"I don't see it," he called.

"It's probably dead," Kellach answered as he stepped over the wolves.

Driskoll looked back at Kellach, who had picked something up from the floor and was examining it. "What is it?" Driskoll asked.

"It looks like a piece of clay—pottery, maybe. It's broken

anyway," Kellach said, tossing it side. "Probably an incense holder or something."

Driskoll continued looking, but the snake was nowhere to be seen.

"It's not here," Moyra yawned. "Why don't we just go home?"

Driskoll was about to turn around when he saw another, larger piece of broken pottery. Something green lay beneath it. He gently lifted the pottery piece, revealing an elegant green snake about twenty inches long. Its eyes were open, but it lay perfectly still, clinging to the tile floor.

Driskoll reached for the snake, but Moyra grabbed his hand.

"Didn't you hear what I said?" she hissed. "I thought that snake was dead this morning, but it bit me."

Driskoll looked at her for a moment, then turned to the snake.

"Come on, he looks harmless."

Moyra still held his hand tight.

"It's definitely dead," Kellach put in. "Whatever burned the wolves probably got to this thing too." Driskoll hadn't noticed that Kellach had been standing there for some time.

"But he doesn't show any signs of being burned," Driskoll said, examining the long, scaly body. He reached out and peeled the snake away from the floor.

"Feels cold," he murmured, holding the little reptile in his hands. "I wonder what—" but he stopped as the snake quivered slightly. It turned its head to look up at him.

"Look!" Driskoll nearly shouted. "He's not dead. And . . . and he smiled at me!"

Kellach snorted. "Oh for the love of mermaids, it did not smile at you. It's probably getting ready to bite you."

Driskoll ignored him. "I'm taking him home," he announced. "I've always wanted a pet snake. I'll name him Suma, after the great bard warrior."

Moyra stood up. "Are you kidding?" Her eyes were wide with disbelief. "How do you know that thing's not poisonous?"

Driskoll stared down at the tiny green snake. "How could something so little and cute be poisonous?" Driskoll asked.

"You've definitely caught this disease," Moyra grumbled. "Your head isn't working."

Kellach reached for the snake. "Let me see it."

Driskoll held it away.

"Come on, Dris, I won't hurt it."

Driskoll sighed and held the snake a tiny bit closer to Kellach.

"Blech," Moyra said under her breath.

Kellach stared hard at the snake. "It's definitely dead."

"He's not dead," Driskoll shot back. "Those wolves just gave him a scare. Or maybe they hurt him. We should take him to a cleric or a healer or something."

"Problem is, all the healers need healing," Kellach observed.

"Not all the healers," Moyra muttered.

Driskoll and Kellach both stared at her. "What do you mean?" Driskoll asked.

Moyra sighed loudly and turned around. "Do I have to explain everything to you two? You can't take a snake to a cleric—clerics heal humans. You have to take it to someone who can heal snakes. You have to take it to an animal healer."

"Do you know anyone like that?" Driskoll asked.

Moyra stared at them and smiled wryly. "What makes you think I would know anyone like that?"

CHAPTER

5

I can't believe I'm doing this," Moyra groaned as they journeyed into the seedier part of the city toward Broken Town. "I'm actually helping you take care of a snake."

Driskoll held the reptile in his hands. He felt a feeble sort of vibrating that he guessed was a heartbeat, but still he worried that the little creature might not make it.

"How far is this place?" he asked as they turned into a bleak and deserted alley.

"A little farther," she said.

"That's what you said five minutes ago when we passed the Skinned Cat," Kellach said. "And I've never been this deep into Broken Town. Where are we?"

"Just never mind," Moyra answered. "Selik is a little secretive about what he does. He keeps a low profile."

"Why? Why does an animal healer need a low profile?" Driskoll asked suspiciously.

"Let me guess." Kellach put in. "He's up to something illegal."

"Now why would you think that?" Moyra asked.

"Because we're heading into the deepest, darkest part of Broken Town," Kellach answered. "Because you know him. And because you seem to know a lot of people who do illegal stuff."

Moyra yawned. "I do have good connections. Doesn't seem like it's ever hurt either of you, though. And anyway, Selik will know exactly what to do. I think you'll like him. He's got some really interesting stuff. "

"You mean he 'steals' interesting stuff," Kellach said.

"Whatever." Moyra shrugged.

"Wait a minute," Driskoll chimed in. "What does a guy with interesting stuff have to do with healing my snake?"

Moyra stopped in front of a narrow space between two abandoned storefronts. "Selik collects art—reptile art," she said. "He loves reptiles. He knows a lot about them, including a few things about healing them. And hey, we're here."

Driskoll peered inside the broken windows. "Which one is Selik's?"

"That one." Moyra pointed at the gap between the buildings.

"He lives there?" Driskoll squeaked, peering into the dark opening, which smelled like something large had recently died in it. "Where's the entrance?"

"This is the entrance," Moyra answered. "Just make sure you keep an eye on the dragon's mouth."

"What dragon?" Driskoll called after her. But Moyra had already slipped through the gap and had disappeared into the darkness. Driskoll shook his head and slid in behind her. He heard

31

Kellach behind him, grumbling something about smelly fish.

They sidled through the blackness, with no light to guide them. All they could do was shuffle farther into the opening.

"Driskoll, move," Kellach ordered.

"I can't see," Driskoll whispered. "And my hands are full with Suma, so I can't hold onto the wall."

"I don't think you want to touch anything in here anyway," Kellach answered. "Just keep walking so we can get through here."

The gap was only about twenty paces long, but it felt like it was a mile across. It finally opened into a weedy old yard that was littered with garbage. Flies hung lazily in the air. Moyra waited in the yard.

Driskoll took a few steps forward into the area. They were behind the two buildings now.

"So, um . . . this is the entrance?" Driskoll asked, looking around. "Isn't this a . . . "

"Garbage dump," Kellach finished. "This place reeks," he said. "I can't believe anyone keeps animals and art within a mile of here."

"It's not what you think," Moyra said. She walked ahead into the yard, stepping over the piles of litter. She seemed to be counting her steps. "Eight, nine, ten." She turned about midway through the yard and faced them.

Driskoll, still standing near the gap, looked at Moyra. "This can't be the right place."

Moyra stared at the building behind him. "Of course it is," she said. "You just have to look carefully." She seemed to be looking for something on the wall.

Driskoll turned and faced it. It was nothing more than a dirty old brick wall covered in layer after layer of grime and graffiti. "What are you looking at?" he asked.

She didn't take her eyes off the building.

"I'm looking for the door. The trick is to look in the mouth."

"What mouth?" Driskoll asked, turning again to look at the wall just behind him.

"What are you talking about, Moyra?" Kellach turned around and stared at the wall too. "There's no door here."

Moyra gave them an exasperated look. "You can't see it from there," she said. "You have to come back here to get the full effect."

Driskoll and Kellach looked at each other. They each took a step, but Moyra held up her hand. "Did you count your paces?" she asked. "You have to count ten paces."

The boys shook their heads.

"Does stepping over a dead rat count as one pace or two?" Driskoll asked.

Moyra made a face. "Just come back here and help me find the door."

Driskoll counted ten paces and found himself standing next to Moyra.

"Now turn around and face the building, like I'm doing," she commanded.

Kellach saluted and turned. Driskoll did the same, without the salute, since he was still holding Suma. He looked at the wall and shrugged. "It's a wall, Moyra. Just the back of a smelly old build—"

Driskoll watched in amazement as the graffiti and grime faded away before his eyes. Now he could see the red bricks as if they were brand new. They seemed to be moving into a pattern. Now they looked like . . . scales. Soon Driskoll could make out a long tail and wings. He wasn't looking at the back wall of an old abandoned building anymore. He was looking at a giant red dragon. It stared at the three of them menacingly, and to Driskoll's very great surprise, it raised its wings and opened its mouth.

Driskoll jumped and reached for his sword.

"Relax, troll brains, it's just a painting," Moyra laughed. "But it's a painful one if you don't find the door."

"I still don't see a door," Driskoll said.

Moyra sighed. "Weren't you listening? You have to look at the mouth. The door moves. Sometimes it's just between its legs, or on its tail. But mostly, the door's in the mouth. Once you spot it, you have to run to it. But you have to be careful because the door disappears fast. If you're not quick enough, you'll run into a solid wall."

"So we have to run right up into this dragon?" Driskoll looked at her like she was crazy.

"I told you, it's just some sort of magical painting," Moyra answered. She pointed at it. "There. See it? The door."

Driskoll turned to look. The painted dragon had bent its head to study them.

"I don't see any door," Driskoll said.

Moyra took off running.

"She's heading straight for the dragon," Driskoll yelled.

"She's crazy," Kellach muttered.

Moyra was moving fast, right for the dragon's mouth. Driskoll looked and between the sharp teeth, he could see a huge red tongue. No wait, it was a red door. And seconds before Moyra got to it, the red door opened. Driskoll's jaw dropped as Moyra ran straight into the dragon's mouth and through the open door.

The dragon clamped its mouth shut, and the door and Moyra were gone.

"Moyra!" Driskoll shouted. "Where are you?"

"I get it," Kellach said. "It's really just a brick wall with a door that can be moved magically. But when I step forward, I can't see it anymore." Kellach walked a few paces ahead and Driskoll followed. The dragon moved out of focus, and again, it was the back of a building.

The boys took two steps back and the dragon appeared again.

"Aha!" Kellach shouted, and he charged toward the dragon. He scooted directly in between the dragon's legs, and in the next moment he had disappeared.

Driskoll stared at the dragon. It was looking between its legs, as if wondering how Kellach had gotten through there.

"Come on, Dris," Kellach's voice called from somewhere inside the dragon. "Just find the door."

"I still don't see any—wait a minute." Driskoll studied the dragon. He could have sworn he saw another red door in the middle of its body. But it disappeared as the dragon turned to look at him again. Puffs of smoke billowed out of its nose.

"Wait," he called. "I think I just saw it. And there it is again." He would have to move fast. He looked at the little snake in his hands. "Don't worry, I'll take care of you," he said, and he slipped Suma in his pocket.

He looked back at the dragon and tried to find the door. There it was again, at the tip of the tail.

"I can't believe I'm doing this," he shouted as he ran straight toward the dragon. He kept his eye on the small door. But a second later, the door was gone.

Thud.

He bounced back into a pile of old pots.

He looked up. The dragon had disappeared and all he could see was solid brick wall. There was no door anywhere.

"Come on, Driskoll, quit fooling around," Kellach called from the other side.

"I'm not fooling around," he howled as he climbed out of the pots and checked the snake inside his pocket. "I'm trying to get in."

Once he was sure Suma was okay, Driskoll counted ten paces to the back of the yard again. He could have sworn the dragon was snickering at him.

"Oh shut up," he said, glaring at it. He squinted and stared hard. The door was again in the dragon's hide. Then it disappeared for a moment and showed up in its mouth. It stayed there for a few seconds, and went back to the spot in between its front legs. Then it went back to the hide again.

I get it, he thought. It's a pattern. Driskoll counted the number of seconds he had at each spot. He figured he had eight seconds to get there. He watched the door appear and disappear one more time just to be sure he had counted the right number of seconds and then he was ready.

Just as the door disappeared from the dragon's mouth, he took off running, straight for the solid wall between its legs—that was where the door would be next.

He picked up his pace, but the door hadn't yet appeared. Had he moved too fast? But this close, he couldn't tell. It was just a brick wall again. He closed his eyes and braced for impact with the wall. He kept running . . . directly into an open doorway.

Someone grabbed him. "Nice of you to join us finally," Kellach said.

Driskoll was out of breath and exhausted. He put his hands on his knees. "What is that all about?" he panted.

"I told you," Moyra said. "Selik likes art."

"That's not my idea of art," Driskoll complained, rubbing his shoulder where he had crashed into the wall. "Well, come on." Kellach was already walking away. "Let's get this over with."

"Follow me," Moyra cut in front of him and led them down a dark, downward sloping hall.

They stopped in front of an open archway.

"What, no dragons?" Driskoll asked.

"Oh just wait," Moyra laughed. "And anyway, Selik figures if you can find his shop and make it past the dragon painting, a simple locked door isn't going to stop you."

She led them under the archway into a dimly lit room, where a huge black dragon crouched in the middle of the tiled floor. This was no painting. It eyed them suspiciously, and its mouth was open wide.

"Don't worry. This one's a statue," Moyra muttered. "And it doesn't move."

Driskoll stared at the dragon. It was so realistic he half

expected flames to come pouring out of its open mouth any minute now. But the dragon remained perfectly still.

Driskoll tried to draw his eyes away from the dragon, but he had a funny feeling it was watching him as he circled the room.

But there were all kinds of interesting things to look at besides the dragon model. Kellach was fascinated by the stacks of expensive-looking books piled high on a table in one corner. Moyra fingered several lovely baskets with intricate patterns worked into them.

But the room's most striking features were its walls. Made entirely of rock, each wall formed a huge floor-to-ceiling mural painted directly on the rock. And while the dragon painting outside was more lifelike than Driskoll would have preferred, these were one-dimensional, to Driskoll's great relief.

The paintings—all in earth tones of sienna, charcoal, and blood red—represented snakes of all kinds. Driskoll followed the murals around the room. They seemed to tell a story. The first wall showed humans pulling huge stone blocks on rollers up a steep grade. Snakes and some other creatures—with bodies of humans but with scaly skin and large, unblinking eyes—stood watching the work. Driskoll noticed that these snakes and snakelike creatures were far bigger than any of the humans in the pictures.

On the next wall, the snakelike creatures were throwing clay on pottery wheels. A real doorway was stuck in the middle of the painting.

The third wall showed a giant black snake surrounded by several smaller snakes. And there was an inscription on it. It said, "To Selik, on your birthday. From Fosh."

The fourth picture was hidden behind a collection of clay pots. They were stacked to the ceiling in several rows. There must have been thousands of pots.

Moyra yawned loudly as Driskoll reached out to touch one of the pots.

A tanned hand grabbed his arm.

CHAPTER

6

I t's okay, Selik," Moyra said. "He's with me."

Selik loosened his grasp on Driskoll's arm, and Driskoll turned and looked at him. He was tall and muscular, with a deeply tanned face and large green eyes. He wore a sort of loose-flowing brown tunic and he carried a delicate china bowl filled with red apples.

He eyed Driskoll suspiciously.

"Sons of the captain of the watch," he murmured, taking in Kellach as well. "Everything here is perfectly legal, you know."

"They're not here to turn you in, Selik," Moyra assured him in a calm voice. "They're with me."

Selik cocked his head toward her. "They're with you, eh?" he said, offering her an apple from the bowl. "Not sure I can trust you either. Remember the so-called dragon ring your father sold me last week? The one he said was magical? Oh, it was magical all right. Turned into a lizard and ran away."

Moyra tried to suppress a giggle as she took the apple. "That was in exchange for the painting you said was done in squid ink. It was just blueberry stains."

"Ahem," Selik cleared his throat and looked away. He leaned against the black dragon. "How is your father these days? I was hoping he could help me get rid of this worthless piece of junk."

Moyra bit into her apple. "What's wrong with the dragon? I've always liked it."

"You want it? It's yours. It's been my fireplace for years—you know, a fire-breathing dragon. But now I can't get a spark out of it."

He shivered. "What am I going to do this winter without a fireplace?"

Moyra looked at Kellach. "Maybe you can help." She turned back to Selik. "He's an apprentice wizard, you know."

Selik nodded at Kellach. "I've heard about you," he said. "You're welcome to try out some of your magic on this old boy."

Kellach gave Driskoll and Moyra an important look and stooped to examine the mouth of the dragon.

They all watched as Kellach straightened up. He closed his eyes and raised his arms. Seconds later, a puff of flames shot from the dragon's mouth.

"Oh well done," Selik cried. "Excellent job. You truly are a powerful wizard."

Kellach bowed. "Thank you," he said brightly.

"Have an apple," Selik said, holding out the bowl. "Take as many as you want." Kellach took one as Selik beamed at him. Driskoll tapped his foot.

"Ahem," Driskoll coughed in Moyra's direction.

"Oh, right," she said. "And Driskoll has something to show you."

Driskoll reached into his pocket and pulled out the snake. Selik, who was still smiling warmly at Kellach, turned to the snake and his expression changed. Suma squirmed.

"Where did you find him?" Selik asked.

"Well, that was a little strange," Driskoll said. "He was in St. Cuthbert's. There were a bunch of dire wolves and they had him surrounded. I think they were going to kill him."

"Hmm," Selik rubbed his chin. "And how did you children manage to save it from a pack of dire wolves?" He turned to Kellach. "No doubt you used some of that magic of yours, eh?"

Kellach grinned.

"Can you help my snake?" Driskoll asked. "I think he's hurt."

"He doesn't look hurt to me," Selik said, pointing at the snake. It was coiling itself around Driskoll's arm.

"Hey, it is still alive," Moyra announced.

"And in perfectly good health," Selik added. "He seems quite attached to you, boy." He searched Driskoll's face with his large green eyes.

"There have been lots of snakes around lately," Moyra said. "We saw tons of them at the cathedral. Do you know anything about why there would be so many snakes lately?"

Selik shrugged. "It's been rather warm. That could be the reason."

"Of course," Driskoll said. "Snakes are cold-blooded, right? The heat is bringing them out." The little snake crawled up onto

Driskoll's shoulder and looked around. Driskoll beamed.

Kellach stepped forward. "Driskoll wants to keep this thing as his pet. Is that safe?"

"Yeah, is it poisonous?" Moyra interrupted.

"Snakes can be dangerous," Selik said. "But your friend's snake is perfectly harmless—just an ordinary garden snake." He looked at the snake for a moment and then at Driskoll. "You'll make a fine snake keeper. Just remember what you said earlier. Snakes are cold-blooded. Keep him someplace warm."

He reached for one of the tightly woven baskets on a table nearby. "Finest construction," he said, running his fingers along the patterns. "It's a snake home that is a work of art in itself." He removed the lid and Driskoll looked inside. The basket was filled with fine sand, and a smooth gray rock jutted out from the middle.

"Thank you." Driskoll reached for the basket, but Selik drew it away.

"That'll be twelve coppers," he said.

"For a basket?" Driskoll was shocked. "I can get the same thing in the square for two coppers."

Selik shrugged. "Nasty construction, those," he said. "Made from troll grass. One minute it's a basket, the next it's strangling you in your bed."

"Really?" Driskoll looked wide-eyed at him.

Moyra rolled her eyes. "No, it's not true," she whispered. "He's bargaining with you. You have to make him cut the price."

Driskoll reached into his pocket. He had been saving for months to buy a pet, and he had exactly twelve coppers. He pulled the money out and laid it on the table next to the basket.

"Driskoll, no," Moyra pleaded. "You're overpaying."

"Nonsense," Selik said. "You won't buy a finer basket anywhere. And a pet needs a comfortable home." Selik pocketed the coins with a look at Moyra. She shook her head at him.

Selik sighed and looked back at Driskoll. "The girl is right, boy," he said. "You really should learn how to bargain. Since I feel sorry for you, I'll throw these into the deal." Selik moved to the corner where the clay pots were piled and came back with three small pots, which he placed carefully inside the basket.

"What are those for?" Driskoll asked.

"The pots are for food. A snake has to eat, you know. You can keep food fresh in these."

"It's still a bad deal," Moyra said in a low voice, looking hard at Selik.

He shrugged. "Every young person must learn certain rules in life. And if it's up to me to be the teacher, so be it."

"Hmm," Moyra paused and looked behind him. "I've never noticed that painting before." She pointed at the wall mural. "Is it new?"

Selik turned toward the painting, and Driskoll thought he saw Moyra move quickly behind him.

Selik turned back to face them. "Yes, it was commissioned for me," he said, eyeing Moyra quickly. "By a client."

Kellach examined the painting. "'To Selik, on your birthday. From Fosh.' Is that your client?" he asked.

Selik thought for a moment. "Yes. He's another, er . . . snake keeper. A great one, in fact. You might say he's the father of all snake keepers."

CHAPTER

7

Driskoll barely noticed the filth and garbage around him as he emerged from the back door. He was too busy trying to carry the large basket, which had looked much smaller in Selik's shop. Now that he was carrying it, it felt about as large and heavy as a bushel full of apples.

Suma didn't help much. The little snake kept poking his head out and trying to shimmy out of the basket.

"What is that?" Kellach asked in a harsh voice from behind him. Driskoll looked at Moyra, who was leafing through a handsome leatherbound book. The letter *Y* was stitched into the cover.

Moyra nodded over her shoulder in the direction they had just come from.

"You stole a book from him?"

"Shh!" Moyra put her finger to her lips. Then she looked at Driskoll. "Listen. You got cheated and Selik knows it. He should keep a better eye on his things if he's going to cheat someone."

"Then why are you whispering about it?" Kellach asked.

45

She ignored him. "I can get a good price on this book for you, Dris. It should make up for the twelve coppers."

But Driskoll was struggling with Suma, who had crawled into his pocket. "I'm not . . . interested."

Moyra shrugged and dropped the book in her bag.

Kellach glared at her. "But why did you have to steal something from him? He didn't do anything to you."

Moyra looked away. "It's thieves' honor," she said. "He expects me to steal something. He'd probably be insulted if I didn't."

"You're making this up," Kellach said.

"Can we just get home?" Driskoll whined. "I want to make Suma as comfortable as possible. He's been through a lot today."

"Sure," Kellach said. "It's past lunchtime too. Let's get something to eat on the way.

They walked in silence to Main Square, again passing the Cathedral of St. Cuthbert. They were all so busy looking at the red sashes of the cathedral and studying the still sleeping watcher, they barely noticed that they were passing under one of the massive statues out front.

Cymric the Terrible's statue overlooked the street and stood over ten feet tall on a large pedestal. At one time, a long sword extended from his massive arm, but the sword had been broken off in the battle following the Sundering of the Seal.

Now all that hung from Cymric's huge arm was some ancient, abandoned black cloak.

"Well, I'm glad you've finally got yourself a pet," Kellach said as they passed beneath the statue's arm. "Even if it is a snake—" He stopped as the cloak fell from the statue and landed on him.

Kellach grabbed it, but the cloak writhed and hissed.

Driskoll realized it wasn't a cloak at all.

"Snake!" he yelled. "Get off, you big—"

Kellach tried to raise his arms to perform a spell, but the black serpent was coiling itself around him, and Kellach was starting to gag. Driskoll put down the basket and joined Kellach's struggle. Moyra screamed, but it was all too late. Kellach shuddered and fell to the ground.

A second later, there was a flash like lightning, and the black snake unwound itself and fell away from Kellach in haze of dirty black smoke.

"Kellach! Are you all right?" Driskoll cried. Moyra dropped down next to him.

Kellach was lying on the ground, perfectly still.

"Oh, Kellach, please answer," Moyra cried.

Kellach's eyelids fluttered and he slowly opened his eyes. He squinted up at Driskoll.

"Are you okay?" Moyra asked. "Did it bite you?"

Kellach touched his forehead. "I'm not sure," he said. "Something . . . happened. I just don't know . . . what it was."

Driskoll looked at Kellach's neck. A strange red scar was forming there, and the skin around it was red too. "Kellach," he said, panicking. "You've been bitten." He looked briefly at the snake on the ground.

Orange flames wrapped around the snake and smoke rose from it. The kids stared as the black body sizzled and shrank. Soon there was nothing left but a long, thick line of ashes and smoke.

"It's just like what happened to the wolves," Moyra said slowly.

Kellach shifted a little and Driskoll helped him up.

"I'm okay," he said, rubbing his neck. "I felt a sharp pain. But . . ."

"But what?" Moyra asked.

Kellach gazed at her. "Then it was gone. I don't really feel anything right now. But that snake . . . I didn't do any magic to it. How did it just burn up like that?"

Moyra suddenly yawned.

"Is this boring you?" Driskoll snapped.

"Well no, but we should get Kellach home."

"I'm fine," Kellach said, getting up. Driskoll went to pick up the basket and noticed that Suma wasn't in it.

"Right there," Moyra said, pointing.

The little green snake lay coiled on the ground. Its head was in striking position, and it was glaring at the ashes of the snake.

"It almost looks like Suma attacked the snake," Kellach said slowly.

Driskoll shook his head. "How could an ordinary little garden snake do something like that?"

🗡 🗡 🗡 🗡 🗡

"That's odd," Driskoll said as they walked in the front door. "What's Dad doing home in the middle of the day?" He put down the basket and slipped Suma inside his jacket pocket. They all went to the door of the study, which was open.

They peeked inside. Torin sat at his desk, his chin cupped in his hand. In his other hand, he held a torn and moldy scroll. Driskoll couldn't tell if his eyes were open or closed.

The boys inched toward their father's desk while Moyra remained at the door of the study.

"Dad?" Kellach asked.

"What?" Torin started and blinked at them.

Kellach came up next to him. "Are you all right, Dad?"

Torin yawned and stretched his arms. "Mmpfh? Just . . . uh, tired." He blinked at the scroll in front of him.

"Dad!" Driskoll tapped him on the shoulder. "Kellach's been hurt."

Torin grunted.

"I'm fine," Kellach insisted.

Driskoll ignored him. "A snake bit him near the cathedral," he continued breathlessly.

"Snake?" Torin asked, his bloodshot eyes widening. Driskoll explained how the snake had attacked Kellach and then fell to the ground in flames.

"Dad?" He asked at the end of the story. Torin had closed his eyes again.

Torin jumped. "But Zendric said it wasn't inevitable," he said.

"Huh?" All three kids asked at once.

"What are you talking about?" Kellach asked.

"Maybe he should get some rest," Moyra said quietly from the doorway.

"Right," Torin answered. He got up and mumbled something about Zendric being inevitable. The kids stared at each other as Torin shuffled toward the door of his office.

"Oh, and Dad," Driskoll called after him. "I got a pet."

"That's great, son," Torin said, and he left the room.

CHAPTER

8

They followed Torin to the front room and watched him trudge up the stairs, his head hanging forward on his chest.

Kellach looked at Driskoll "Have you ever seen Dad go to bed in the middle of the day?"

Driskoll didn't answer. He was too busy fumbling with Suma and the basket.

"It's not a bad idea," Moyra yawned. "Maybe I'll catch a few winks too." She slinked over to a corner and curled up like a sleepy cat on a worn-out cushion. She closed her eyes and lay perfectly still.

Kellach stared at her in amazement as Driskoll searched the room for a cozy spot to put Suma's basket. He rested it in front of the hearth and sat down next to it.

Kellach sat down by the window. "Well, this is very strange," he muttered.

"Yeah," Driskoll answered, picking up his snake. "Did you

notice how he has these neat little black markings all around his face?"

Kellach rolled his eyes. "I'm not talking about the snake."

He got up and inspected his neck in the mirror that hung above the fireplace.

Driskoll sighed. He didn't know why, but he somehow felt responsible for the snake attack. As if by carrying the basket with his new pet, he had attracted the huge serpent. "So you're feeling okay?" he asked.

"Yeah," Kellach answered. "A little tired, maybe."

Suma had slithered up to him, his tiny tongue darting. Driskoll chuckled at the sight. "Did you ever notice a snake's tongue is shaped like a Y?"

"Is it?" Kellach said, half listening.

"Yeah, some people call it a forked tongue."

"As fascinating as that is," Kellach said, looking away from the mirror, "let's get back to the problem at hand. There's some kind of disease spreading, and Dad's asleep in the middle of the day. I think he may be infected."

"But how?" Driskoll asked.

Kellach studied Suma.

Driskoll looked from Kellach to the snake. "Oh come on, Kellach. You don't think Suma has anything to do with this, do you? You said yourself he's the one who attacked that snake at the cathedral."

"I didn't say that exactly," Kellach said. "But don't you think it's pretty odd that snakes are suddenly everywhere just as every-one is falling ill with this sleeping sickness?"

"It's the hot weather," Driskoll replied. "Remember what Selik said—"

"Didn't Moyra say a snake bit her this morning?" Kellach interrupted. He looked at Moyra, who was sound asleep on her cushion with her arm drawn over her face. Kellach took her hand gently and studied it. "Look at this."

On the back of Moyra's hand, just below her thumb, there was a strange scar. It was a long line that split into two.

"I bet that's where the snake bit her," Kellach said. "It looks a lot like what I've got on my neck right now."

"Well that doesn't look like a snakebite to me," Driskoll said. "Where are the teeth marks? It's just a weird line that splits in two, like . . . "

"Like what?"

"Like the letter *Y*," he said quietly.

"Didn't you just say a snake's tongue is shaped like the letter *Y*?" Kellach asked. "That could mean the scar was made by the snake, maybe even your—"

"Would you quit blaming Suma for this, Kellach?" Driskoll sighed. "You're just jealous you don't have a pet like I do," he said quietly, opening the basket and taking the clay pots out. "And Suma is the best pet I could have asked for." The snake crawled right inside the basket.

"That's funny," Kellach said. "Your snake didn't want anything to do with the basket until you took those clay pots out."

Kellach picked up one of the clay pots, held it up to his forehead, and closed his eyes. Then he opened his eyes and put the pot back on the floor. "Definitely magical," he said. He tapped his chin. "So why would something that holds food be magical?

And why was Selik so interested in getting rid of them?"

"Maybe the pots bring food to snakes magically?" Driskoll suggested weakly.

Kellach was about to answer, but there was a knock at the door.

Kellach opened the door and saw a familiar face.

"Sergeant Gwinton," Kellach said. "What are you doing here?"

Gwinton rubbed his neck. He had the same look that Torin had—bloodshot eyes, pale skin. He didn't speak.

"Do you want to come in?" Kellach asked.

Gwinton nodded and staggered inside. "I'm here for Torin," he said.

"Torin is, uh, upstairs," Driskoll said. He could see that Gwinton was trying hard to keep his eyes open.

"But you must tell him," Gwinton said.

"Tell him what?"

There was a long pause while Gwinton tried to gather his strength. He swallowed hard. "Tell him," he said slowly. "Tell him that the disease has spread all over the city."

9

Driskoll hurriedly closed the door. Kellach dragged Gwinton to the sofa near the fireplace. They found a few more cushions, and Kellach lifted the old watcher's head while Driskoll tucked the pillows underneath.

"Whatever this sickness is, it looks like Gwinton's got it himself," Kellach said.

"So it's definitely some kind of sleeping sickness," Driskoll added.

"And that means Dad's got it, and Moyra too."

"And the rest of the city, according to Gwinton."

Kellach slapped his forehead. "Of course. The watcher in front of the cathedral. He wasn't sleeping on the job. He has this disease, whatever it is."

Driskoll stared at Moyra's pale face and listened to her shallow breathing. "What's going to happen to them?" he asked, trying not to sound frightened.

"That's what makes this so frustrating." Kellach clenched

his fists. "We don't know what's going to happen."

"Maybe there's something in one of your books," Driskoll suggested.

Kellach waved at the bookshelves lining the walls of the sitting room. "I have books about spells and magic," he said. "Not diseases. Zendric's never taught me anything about that. And if we don't figure this out soon, we're going to be asleep too. Maybe forever."

Driskoll stopped. "What makes you say that?"

Kellach put his hands on his hips. "Think about it, Dris. Dad suspected foul play, right? Whoever is doing this, they've got a reason for it. I don't think they're just putting everyone to sleep because we need the rest."

"So we've got to think of something, right?"

"Right," Kellach answered. "And we'd better do it fast."

Driskoll brightened. "Wait a minute. Didn't Gwinton say that Dad was already investigating this disease? Maybe he has some clues."

"Good idea," Kellach said. "Remember when Dad was in his study a little while ago? He was reading some old, moldy scroll."

"Right," Driskoll agreed as they walked into Torin's study.

The boys looked at the wooden desk, which wasn't as big or as messy as the one in Torin's office at Watchers' Hall. Still, there were quite a few scrolls scattered across it.

Kellach waved his arms and the scrolls and parchments flew into four neat little piles at each corner of the desk.

Driskoll held out his arms. "Now why couldn't you have done that today?"

Kellach shrugged and searched the desk. "Aha," he yelled, picking up a scroll tinged with green at the edges.

"What's it say?" Driskoll asked.

"It's a search warrant . . . Of course!" Kellach set the scroll back on the desk and headed for the door.

Driskoll raced after his brother. "Wait! Where are you going?"

"Just follow me. I'll explain on the way."

* * * * *

"Oh no . . . " Driskoll said as they approached Main Square. "We're not going back to St. Cuthbert's, are we? I'm not going back there."

Kellach sighed. "Listen, remember this morning? Dad was hunting for a search warrant. It was the same warrant I found on his desk. Do you remember where they were going?"

Driskoll frowned. "They weren't going to get me a pet. That's all I remember."

"Come on, Dris." Kellach was almost shouting now. "They were going to the blacksmith's, and that's what the search warrant was for."

"Ohhhh." Driskoll's eyes lit up. "You're right. I do remember Gwinton mentioning the blacksmith's shop."

"Uh huh," Kellach said. "And that's where we're headed. If Dad was investigating this disease by searching the blacksmith's shop, it's possible we might find a clue there that will help him."

"And Moyra and Gwinton," Driskoll added.

"Right." Kellach shaded his eyes from the bright sun and

looked around the empty cobblestone street. "Have you noticed anything strange around here?"

Driskoll listened. The usual squawks and cries of haggling vendors and bargain hunters were gone. "It's so quiet." He lowered his voice.

Kellach stepped up to the baker's cart, which was draped with red sashes. A watcher, still holding some of the silken fabric, lay in front of the cart.

"He must have fallen asleep while he was putting up the quarantine sashes," Driskoll muttered.

"I wonder where the elf maiden is," Kellach said, stepping over the watcher. He stopped abruptly on the other side of the cart.

"What is it?" Driskoll yelled, running around the side. He stopped when he saw the elf maiden who sometimes sold them sugary treats from behind her cart. She lay perfectly still in the dirt, her eyes shut tight, her face pale and drawn.

Kellach leaned toward the tiny, graceful figure. "She's breathing," he said, standing. "Come on. The blacksmith's is just across the way."

"I was just there yesterday," Driskoll said, stumbling to catch up with Kellach. "Grayson sharpened my sword for free."

Kellach smirked. "I'm sure it was in dire need, after all that sword fighting you've been doing with the mirror."

"Oh very funny. That's known as practicing. It's for people who want to actually get good at something."

"Yeah," Kellach said. "And if you keep practicing, maybe someday you'll actually beat that mirror."

Driskoll made a face as they passed under the metal sign

bearing an etched anvil. He read the words inscribed on the sign that he'd seen so many times before:

> Blacksmith's Shop and Historical Site.
> Oldest Working Chimney in Curston—
> Built Before the Sundering of the Seal.

Driskoll had spent many afternoons inside the shop, talking with Grayson, the blacksmith's son and apprentice. They shared a fascination with the old fireplace and chimney, which was built on an ancient stone platform in the very middle of the shop. Grayson had often told Driskoll he'd heard strange noises coming from beneath the fireplace at night.

"Probably ghosts of the old adventurers who broke the seal and unleashed the monsters," Grayson added, the twinkle in his eye lighting up his grimy face. "Or maybe the monsters themselves."

Then Grayson's father would tell him to stop talking nonsense and get back to work, and Driskoll would watch while Grayson pounded out a metal hinge or key from a scrap of red-hot metal.

But there was no sign of Grayson or his father now as Driskoll peered in the big front window, which took up almost half of the front wall.

"The place is a mess," Kellach murmured.

"That's strange," Driskoll said. "Grayson usually keeps things pretty tidy."

They slipped over to the open front door and edged gingerly around a huge iron vat, big enough for Driskoll and Kellach to take a bath in at the same time (although they would never even think of such a thing). The vat had been pushed over and sat on its side just inside the doorway.

"Looks like there's been a scuffle," Kellach whispered. Driskoll nodded. Water had spilled out of the vat and spread all over the wooden planks in the floor. Hammers, hinges, and other metal tools were scattered across the shop.

Picking his way around the overturned tables and benches, Driskoll headed for the fireplace in the center. Two long tables had been knocked over, forming a kind of low wall halfway around the fireplace, and the big leather bellows that Grayson often let Driskoll pump into the flames lay on the floor nearby.

"The fire's out," Driskoll observed, running his fingers through the ashes. "The ashes are still warm, but it looks like the fire's been out for a while."

The ashes fell to the floor, covering something Driskoll hadn't noticed before. He jumped.

"Kellach!" He whispered frantically. "There's a hand down here."

Kellach darted over just as Driskoll realized the hand belonged to the blacksmith, who lay stretched out in front of the fireplace, sound asleep.

"But where's Grayson?" Driskoll asked once he had calmed down a little.

Kellach walked around the fireplace, looking at the floor. "What do you think of this?" he asked.

Driskoll looked at the floor around the massive brick fireplace. "Looks like it's been swept recently," he said.

They followed the ashes and sweep marks toward the back of

the shop, past the little ladder that led upstairs to the loft where Grayson and his father lived to the small door that led outside.

"Whew!" Driskoll said as he stepped out. "Something stinks!" And he would have tripped on the source of the horrible smell, but he happened to look down. The sweep marks on the ground led directly to a pile of dead snakes.

"How many do you think there are?" Driskoll asked, curling his lip.

"Hard to say," Kellach said. "But you can tell from the way they're so carelessly piled here that they met a pretty violent end. I wonder if they had something to do with the scuffle inside."

Driskoll looked around. He was just about to wonder again where Grayson was when he saw him just behind the pile of snakes, sound asleep in the dirt, his arms wrapped around a broom.

Kellach saw him too. "I guess we know who swept these things outside," he said.

"Ugh," Driskoll groaned. "Come on, Kellach, let's move Grayson away from here."

"Just a minute." Kellach bent to pick up a small piece of clay near the pile of snakes. "Interesting," he muttered, turning it over in his hands. "Looks like a broken piece of pottery."

"Very nice," Driskoll said. "But what about Grayson?"

Kellach pocketed the shard, and with a wave of his arm, he levitated Grayson up and through the back door. Driskoll followed them inside and watched as Kellach, with a slow movement of his hand, gently directed the floating boy through the shop. He set him down next to his father in front of the fireplace.

Driskoll gazed at the sleeping blacksmith and his son. They

were both on their backs with their mouths wide open, breathing evenly.

"They look peaceful," Driskoll said. He looked at the two grimy but honest faces. "I'm having a hard time thinking of these two being involved in any kind of foul play."

Kellach nodded and looked toward the back door. "Judging from those sweep marks, I'd say that Grayson swept those dead snakes outside from around the fireplace. But what were snakes doing here in the first place?"

Driskoll was about to answer when a loud crash out in the street stopped him. He reached for his sword. He heard hoof beats and clanking armor. It sounded like an army of knights on horseback was charging down the street.

Both boys ran to the open door, crouching noiselessly behind the overturned vat.

Crash. Driskoll watched a merchant's cart twice his size tumble down the street.

Clank. Clank. Crash. Another cart hurtled forward, landing directly in front of the vat. Driskoll thought wildly of giants. Only something really big and really strong could throw a cart the size of three men down the street.

They peered over the edge of the vat. More carts tumbled in a cloud of dust as the clanking and galloping drew nearer.

In a few seconds, the army or giant or whatever it was would be directly in front of the shop where the boys hid. Driskoll, his heart pounding, clutched his sword.

The galloping slowed to a walk in front of the shop next door, and a huge shadow, nearly thirty feet long, darkened the street in front of them.

Driskoll and Kellach, with only the tiniest bit of their faces visible as they peered up from behind the vat, didn't dare move, even as the slow hoof beats shook the earth around them.

And when the source of the noise and shadow became visible, Driskoll's pounding heart nearly stopped.

Not a giant, not an armored knight, but a little of both. A monstrous creature—an inhuman creature—the likes of which they had never seen, had stopped directly in front of them.

With the body of a horse and the head and torso of a man, the thing was easily ten feet tall. A spiked iron chain hung from its forearms. But where a natural creature had muscle and bone, its golden inner workings were gears, axles, rods and pins— and they were all strangely visible beneath an alabaster armor. Only the creature's metal joints were fully exposed.

It looked like a huge, golden centaur—a very, very dangerous centaur.

The boys ducked low as the thing swiveled its head around with the jerky, mechanized movements of a clockwork creature.

But Driskoll knew this creature was nothing like friendly old Locky, Kellach's tiny clockwork dragon familiar. Friendly creatures did not throw carts down streets.

Driskoll waited for it to start throwing carts again, but it stood rooted to the spot, not making a sound.

Why did it stop here? he thought. What's it waiting for?

Over the sound of his beating heart, Driskoll began to hear a noise: a constant, droning sort of noise almost like a buzzing bee, but unnatural and alien. It took Driskoll a few seconds to realize that it was a voice of some sort, and it was forming words.

Although what those words were, Driskoll had no clue. It was another language, and definitely not a human one.

He looked at Kellach, whose already-frightened face had gone two shades paler.

"What?" Driskoll mouthed.

Kellach put his finger to his lips for silence. Driskoll's heart raced while the creature repeated the same mechanized phrase over and over. And then, as if it had heard or seen something, it stopped.

Driskoll waited for it to pick up its droning sound again, but all was silent. He had a funny feeling they had been detected somehow. He felt sure *something* was watching him, but strangely, the feeling wasn't coming from outside. Something inside the shop—and very close by—was watching him too.

He looked at his brother. Kellach must have felt it too, because he glanced behind him. Driskoll looked too.

A wooden bench had been overturned a few feet behind them. And poking its head above the bench was a large black snake.

Its monstrous yellow eyes flashed back and forth between the boys, and its tongue flickered hungrily.

Great, Driskoll thought. Now what were they going to do? There was a mechanical monster outside and a reptilian monster inside.

The snake must have been aware of the creature on the other side of that vat, and it crouched low to avoid it. But the snake's joy over its two trapped victims mastered it, and it couldn't help itself. It hissed.

Instantly, a ferocious crash boomed over the boys' heads as the iron vat tumbled over, right on top of them.

CHAPTER

10

Driskoll forgot about the snake as he scrambled away. He looked at the vat lying upside down on the floor where he and Kellach had been crouching only seconds ago. Kellach couldn't be anywhere else but underneath. The mechanical creature ambled up onto the vat, squashing it like a pumpkin.

"Kellach!" Driskoll yelled in horror.

But Kellach's reflexes were even faster than his own, and he was already behind Driskoll, grabbing him and pulling him away. They scuttled behind a bench for protection.

The creature galloped over the vat and into the shop. It paused for a moment, and its skull-like face rotated, as if it were looking for something. Driskoll caught a glimpse of two golden eyes swiveling in their sockets like deadly cannonballs ready to fire. There was an intelligence behind those eyes that was unnerving.

Then the beast was on the move again, crushing or throwing everything in its path. The ceiling didn't pose any problem for its height. It easily pushed through the wooden beams with its chained arms as if it were brushing away cobwebs, and threw entire rafters across the room.

Kellach motioned to Driskoll to follow him, and they scooted farther back toward the fireplace where the smith and his son lay.

Kellach looked at Driskoll and did a double take. His jaw dropped in horror as he stared at Driskoll's chest.

"What?" Driskoll hissed, trying to remain calm despite the fact that an anvil had just whizzed past his ear. He looked down at his chest, expecting to see blood or a wound, but all he could see was his Silver Dragon pin. His jacket had torn open when he had dodged the falling vat, and the pin was clearly visible. But why would Kellach be so horrified by a thing Driskoll wore every day?

"Forget the blacksmith," Kellach whispered. He grabbed Driskoll and dragged him back into a corner of the shop. "Stay here," he commanded.

Kellach turned back toward the monster, which was thrashing near the front of the shop. The boy wizard raised his arms in what Driskoll guessed was a spell, and a hammer on the ground next to Kellach began to quiver. It raised itself up into the air as if on an invisible string, and then shot forward.

The hammer hit the creature's forehead squarely, dazing it for a moment. Driskoll cheered silently, but the creature kept moving forward. The hammer hadn't fazed it. Meanwhile, more tools arose at Kellach's command: another bigger hammer, a spade, a poker. They all glanced off the armor, which was deceivingly impenetrable. Soon the air was full of hundreds of metal objects all flying toward the creature: hinges, locks, even nails—anything that wasn't nailed down was flying at it. But everything bounced

66

off and flew wildly around the shop.

Kellach's spell wasn't working. In fact, it was going a little haywire. The creature was unstoppable. Driskoll thought it would be a miracle if the thing didn't trample Grayson and his dad.

Driskoll had had enough. He got up from his corner, raised his sword in the air and charged.

"Driskoll, no!" Kellach swiped at him, but missed.

The creature turned at Kellach's voice and focused on Driskoll, who was near the fireplace, fully exposed and waving his sword.

"No, Dris! Not your sword!" Kellach shouted.

Driskoll felt his sword move in his hand, and he realized with a sudden horror that it was responding to Kellach's spell. He held on tight, but the sword wriggled out of his grip and sailed into the air, directly into the creature's chest. Then it simply fell away as if it were made of rubber. It bounced onto the floor and Driskoll lost sight of his beloved weapon as it blended into the shower of metal tools careening around the shop.

"My sword!" he shouted.

"Get back!" Kellach ran up to Driskoll and pulled him away. "Don't let it see you."

But the creature had already spotted the young swordsman. Driskoll froze. He felt like his insides were melting as the creature's gears ground to a halt and those glowing metal eyes stared at him.

Kellach waved his hands in the air. "I can't stop the spell," he shouted frantically as tools flew around them. But Driskoll hardly heard Kellach. He was staring at the creature. It didn't take its eyes off Driskoll.

Its huge body took up the entire front portion of the shop, blocking the doorway. It took a step toward the boys.

"Run!" Kellach cried, waving his arms.

"What about Grayson?" Driskoll yelled back.

"It's not after him," Kellach shouted. "Come *on*." He tugged at Driskoll and pointed toward the back door. There was a clear path for them to run behind the fireplace and out the back door. But Driskoll couldn't believe Kellach would leave Grayson and his dad alone with this creature. He broke away from Kellach and ran, trying to dodge the shower of tools, toward the front of the fireplace, where Grayson and his dad lay.

The creature took two more steps toward them.

"Driskoll, you idiot!" Kellach scrambled after Driskoll, who crouched near the blacksmith.

"Come on, Kellach, levitate them out of here!" Driskoll shouted as a hammer above him bounced off the chimney. He looked wildly at the creature. It was striding slowly toward them, as if it were playing with them.

Kellach pulled at Driskoll and furiously beat at the air to try and stop the spell. "It doesn't want them," Kellach shouted. "It wants you!"

He gave Driskoll another tug, but an iron spade conked Kellach in the back of the head and he crumpled to the floor next to the blacksmith and Grayson.

The rain of tools stopped suddenly, and Driskoll looked at the gigantic creature. It trotted forward, its upper body crashing through the ceiling rafters. Beams and timbers plummeted to the floor, but the creature didn't notice. Its eyes were fixed on Driskoll, and its mechanized voice began droning again.

Driskoll looked around. Kellach lay unconscious next to the blacksmith and Grayson. The fireplace blocked his way out, but even if he could move, he wasn't about to leave his brother here with this mechanical beast. The only thing left was the fireplace, but there were no tools near it—they had all flown off. All that was left were useless ashes.

Driskoll couldn't think of anything else. He reached into the fireplace. He swept his arms around the ashes, and with all of his strength, pushed them out toward the creature. The ashes blew into the creature's skull-like face. Driskoll grabbed the wooden bellows and tried blowing the ashes up farther into the creature. It stopped momentarily and brushed the feeble little cloud of ash away. But within seconds the cloud was gone and Driskoll wondered why he had even tried. That had done nothing to stop the creature.

"Good idea," Kellach said in a pained voice behind him. He was getting to his feet. The creature was only a few paces away as Driskoll turned around to sweep more ashes out of the fireplace. Kellach, holding one hand to his head, raised his free arm and closed his eyes. An obscuring mist billowed up around them.

A swirling gray haze—mostly magical, but partly ash—surrounded them. They could feel the creature inches away. It had stopped moving.

"I've got Grayson and his dad," Kellach whispered from somewhere in the haze nearby. "Let's get out of here."

Driskoll said nothing but moved in the direction of Kellach's voice. The ashes in the air made him want to cough, but he suppressed it.

An ominous cracking sound echoed just above them, and Driskoll knew it was only a matter of time before the roof, which had been damaged by the creature, would collapse.

He climbed over the fallen furniture, his eyes streaming, listening for Kellach in front of him. The creature did not follow. Somehow Driskoll's ashes and Kellach's obscuring mist had stopped it.

Driskoll felt his way forward and climbed over the iron vat. He stumbled out, coughing and hacking, into the raw sunshine. Through watery eyes, he could see Kellach standing to one side, levitating the blacksmith and Grayson into the street.

Kellach pointed to the sleeping figures behind the elf maiden's cart.

He turned and looked at Driskoll. "I don't like this," he said. "Why isn't it chasing us?" I can't believe that a little bit of ash and mist stopped that thing, but all of those tools didn't."

"I don't know," Driskoll panted. "But it's still in there and that shop's going to come down on it any minute."

Just as he said it, the walls of the shop shuddered. A crack snaked up the big glass window.

"Get down," Kellach yelled, and they both fell to the ground. Driskoll peered up. With an almighty cracking sound, the roof of the blacksmith's shop sank and the walls toppled around it. Little jets of glass streamed out from the window as it shattered and exploded. Driskoll quickly covered his eyes as a sound like an exploding cannon rocked the earth.

Seconds later, Driskoll looked up again. All that was left of the blacksmith's proud shop was the great stone fireplace, its high chimney, and a lot of rubble.

"My sword," Driskoll groaned.

Kellach stared at the ruins. "What?"

"I lost my sword," Driskoll said, getting up. "It's in there." He pointed at the pile of rocks, dust, and broken beams.

"I don't think you're going to find it," Kellach said.

CHAPTER

11

"What was that thing?" Driskoll stared at the ruins of the blacksmith's shop.

Kellach shook his head. "I've never seen anything like it."

Driskoll walked slowly over to the ruins. A long poker stick lay out in front. Driskoll picked it up. "Whatever it was, it's gone now."

"I wouldn't be so sure," Kellach said. "That wasn't a living being. It might be able to rebuild itself. I've heard of things like that from Mechanus."

Driskoll took a step back from the ruins and stared at Kellach. "Who?"

"Mechanus. It's another plane, you know."

"No, I don't know," Driskoll said. "You lost me at the part where you said it could rebuild itself."

But Kellach didn't explain. He was looking from the elf maiden's cart to the deserted shops along the street. "There's not a soul in sight," he murmured. "No one's come running to see what the big explosion was."

"Let's go home," Driskoll said, holding the poker stick. "This is really creepy. And I want to check on Suma . . . "

Kellach glared at him.

" . . . Oh, and uh, Moyra, Dad, and Gwinton too," Driskoll finished.

Kellach nodded at the poker stick in Driskoll's hands. "Is that your new sword?"

"It's better than nothing," Driskoll replied as they turned and headed for home.

■ ■ ▐ ▐ ■

At first Driskoll thought the large brown object on their doorstep was a package. But as they got closer and he saw a face with black markings, he realized with horror that it was a huge snake.

"Hold still," Kellach said quietly.

"I'm not going anywhere," Driskoll murmured.

The unblinking green eyes stared at them as the snake uncoiled itself. It was big, about twice the size of Suma. It watched them as it slid down the steps, along the base of the house, and around the side.

The boys followed carefully, peeking around the side of their house. The snake was gone.

"It disappeared," Driskoll said, letting out a long breath.

"What was that all about?" Kellach asked, scanning the walls of the house.

"I thought it was going to attack," Driskoll said, returning to the front door.

"Me too," Kellach agreed. "But . . . "

"But what?"

"Well, this is going to sound strange," Kellach folded his arms in front of him, "but that thing looked . . . familiar."

"I know what you mean," Driskoll said. "Maybe it was one of those snakes in the cathedral."

"Maybe," Kellach said, sounding unconvinced. "But it reminded me of something else. I'm not sure what."

They went inside. Kellach ran upstairs to check on Torin while Driskoll headed for the living room. There was Gwinton, still asleep on his cushions. Next to him, on another set of cushions, Moyra slept soundly. Neither looked like they had moved.

Driskoll looked in Suma's basket. It was empty.

"Kellach!" Driskoll yelled.

Kellach ran back down the stairs. "What? Are you okay?"

"Suma's gone."

Kellach rolled his eyes. "Is that all? I thought something bad had happened." He knelt near Suma's basket and examined several pieces of broken pottery that lay scattered on the floor. "Strange."

"The pots," Driskoll gasped. "They're broken."

Kellach took the clay piece that he had found at the blacksmith's out of his robes and held it near what was left of the pots. "They're similar, anyway," he said. He glanced at Moyra. "And if you're looking for your snake, it's right here."

Driskoll looked at Moyra just in time to see the snake's back end disappear around her neck. Kellach reached behind Moyra and grabbed Suma behind the snake's head.

"Wait, Kellach! Don't hurt him!"

"Don't hurt him? What about Moyra?" Kellach held the snake tightly. Suma looked limp in his hands.

Driskoll grabbed the snake and studied him while Kellach did the same for Moyra. "I don't see any bite marks," Kellach said. "And she's still breathing."

"What, you think he was trying to hurt her?"

Kellach didn't take his eyes off Moyra. "I don't know what it was doing," he said quietly.

Driskoll looked at the little snake in his hands. He had revived a bit and stared at Driskoll.

Kellach looked up. "I don't know, Driskoll," he said, gesturing with a piece of pottery. "This is really strange."

"Well, Suma's not involved," Driskoll said hotly. "He saved you from that snake in front of the cathedral."

Kellach threw his hands in the air.

Suma squirmed wildly in Driskoll's arms. "Will you cut that out, Kellach? You're bothering him."

Kellach looked from the clay piece in his hands to the snake. He held the piece up to Suma's face, and the snake jumped out of Driskoll's hands and landed on the floor. The creature slithered quickly away.

"Kellach!" Driskoll cried. "What are you doing?"

"Interesting," Kellach breathed. "I wonder if he's the one who smashed the pots."

"Are you crazy?" Driskoll yelled as he picked up Suma and cradled him. "How could a little snake smash all those pots?"

Kellach shrugged. "Well, someone did it, and he's the only one who's been awake here. And he doesn't seem to like those pots."

"Or he's afraid of them," Driskoll added, petting Suma.

"Hmpfh," Kellach grunted and turned toward the bookshelves. "Anyway, I want to find out more about that creature at the blacksmith's." He scanned the spines of the books and muttered to himself. "I wonder why that thing was talking about the Knights."

"What do you mean?"

"Didn't you hear it?" Kellach turned away from the bookshelf.

"Yeah, I heard it," Driskoll answered. "But I didn't know what it was saying. I don't speak . . . whatever that mechanical language is."

Kellach was silent for a moment. Then he pointed at Driskoll's Knights of the Silver Dragon pin.

"You sure you didn't recognize what it was saying?"

Driskoll thought back to the strange voice. "Nope," he said. "Didn't catch a word."

Kellach gazed at him. "It was saying, 'Knights of the Silver Dragon. Where are the Knights of the Silver Dragon?'"

Driskoll's jaw dropped. "It's looking for us? How do you know that's what it said?"

"I know a few words of the Mechanus languages. And I definitely understand words like 'knights' and 'silver dragon.'"

Kellach pointed at Driskoll's chest. "It saw your pin when your coat ripped."

Driskoll looked down at the ornately carved silver pin, and he felt a cold sweat break out on his brow. "Well, thank the gods it's stopped now."

"I wouldn't be so sure." Kellach pulled a book from the shelf.

"I'd still like to know why it was looking for us." He scanned the title of the ragged old volume.

"Dunno," Driskoll said, nuzzling Suma's nose. "Maybe since we're the only ones who aren't asleep, it wants to put us to sleep too." He watched as Suma slithered into his jacket pocket. "You know, Kellach, I've been thinking. That thing was made of metal just like everything else in the blacksmith's shop. And Dad was investigating the blacksmith. Maybe that creature has something to do with the disease."

Kellach flipped through the book. "I'm not so sure, Dris," he said. "What about those dead snakes in the back? What were they doing there? I think Dad and Gwinton went to the blacksmith shop and fought off those snakes. That's why they were piled up in back."

He continued flipping through the book while Driskoll watched Suma.

"Here it is," Kellach said. He held up the book for Driskoll to see. A gold, mechanical-looking centaur-like creature with chains extending from its arms stared out at him from the page. Driskoll stepped back. The thing looked so real he thought it was about to jump right off the page.

Kellach looked at the book again. "'Inevitable . . . '" he read. "'So named because it is inevitable that they find their prey. They are virtually indestructible creatures designed to bring punishment.'"

"Punishment?" Driskoll asked. "Maybe the punishment is this disease—the sleeping disease. And it wants to give it to us too."

"But why would it be punishing everyone in Curston?"

Driskoll thought for a moment. "Well that's easy," he said. "Maybe it wants to punish the town for the Sundering of the Seal. There are plenty of creatures who are pretty angry about all that."

Kellach sighed. "It's possible," he said. "But I think if that thing wanted to punish us, it could just pick us up and toss us all the way to the ruins."

"Wait a minute," Driskoll interrupted. "You say it's called an Inevitable? Didn't Dad say something about Zendric being inevitable?"

"You're right," Kellach said. "Then again, Dad was so tired he could have been talking about anything."

"So what else does the book say?"

Kellach frowned. "That's the problem. There's more, but the next page is missing. Someone tore it out."

"Who would do that?" Driskoll asked.

"How should I know?" Kellach snapped. "Come on. Let's go ask Zendric. If anyone knows about Inevitables, it would be him." He put the book away and started for the door.

"Huh?" Driskoll looked up. "You mean go outside? Into the city? What if that Inevitable thing has rebuilt itself? It'll be after us in a minute."

Kellach shrugged. "Well, we're not going to solve this problem staying inside. And anyway, we should check on Zendric."

"But, Kellach," Driskoll said as he stood up, balancing the snake on his shoulder. "It's not safe."

"I know," Kellach said. "Since when has that ever stopped us?" He stood in front of the door and slowly opened it. He peered outside.

"Do you see anything?" Driskoll whispered. He stood at Kellach's shoulder.

"No," Kellach said. "But it's so quiet. It's almost too quiet."

"Well yeah," Driskoll said impatiently. "Considering that the entire town is asleep, it probably is pretty quiet out there."

"Shhh." Kellach elbowed him in the ribs. "You don't know who or what could be hiding behind the house."

"Let's just get it over with," Driskoll said. He was about to step outside when he felt someone breathing just behind him. He froze. Something clamped his shoulder, and Driskoll yelled loud enough to awaken everyone in Curston.

CHAPTER

12

"M oyra!" Kellach whispered. "You're awake."

Driskoll caught his breath as Moyra's hand fell away from his shoulder. She looked beyond the boys and out the door.

"Yeah," she yawned. "Where are you two going?"

"We're going to Zendric's. It's a long story."

Moyra squinted and blinked at them. "Wouldn't you rather take a nice nap?" she muttered thickly.

Driskoll looked at Kellach. "This is good news, isn't it? It means everyone else might wake up, right?"

Kellach looked serious. "But your snake was on her neck—"

"What?" Moyra's eyes opened a little wider. "Did you say a snake?"

"I think Suma saved her," Driskoll interrupted. "Just like he saved you, Kellach."

Moyra, who couldn't seem to focus on anything for very long, pointed at Gwinton lying on the floor. "What's he doing here?"

Kellach studied her closely. "We can explain on the way to Zendric's. But maybe you're not up for a walk."

"No," Moyra snapped. "I'm not staying here next to Gwinton." She swayed a little and yawned again.

Kellach hesitated. "I don't know, Moyra. You look really tired."

Moyra sat down on her cushion again.

"I don't think she should stay here, Kellach." Driskoll said. "That Inevitable is looking for the Knights. If it comes here . . . well, look at her. How will she defend herself?"

Moyra yawned loudly.

Kellach thought for a moment and tried to suppress a yawn too.

"Oh great, and you were bitten," Driskoll said, the fear rising in his voice. "Now you're going to fall asleep too."

"All right," Kellach said, getting up. "I know something that might help. Keep her awake for a few minutes."

"What?" Driskoll called after him as Kellach headed for the kitchen. "How do I do that?"

Kellach tossed his hands in the air. "Just keep her sitting up with her eyes open."

Driskoll ran after him. "How do I do that?"

Kellach slammed the kitchen door behind him.

Driskoll looked at Moyra, who had moved her cushion as far away from Gwinton as she could. Now she sat and stared at Suma's basket with glazed eyes. Driskoll tiptoed over to her.

"Moyra?"

She stretched. "Mmff," she murmured, getting ready to lie down.

"Uh, come on, Moyra." Driskoll stood several feet away from her. "You have to stay awake for a few minutes."

He took a step closer.

Moyra's head swayed back and forth as she slid deeper into the cushion. "Mm . . . who are you?" she asked dreamily.

He took a few steps closer. "I-I'm Driskoll. Your friend. Remember?"

"Right. Dimball."

"Driskoll."

"Dismall."

"Yeah, whatever. Moyra, you have to stay awake." Driskoll reached out to pat her on the head, but she moved and he pulled his arm back. Her head fell forward onto her chest.

"Kellach?" he called nervously. "Are you almost finished?"

"Just keep her awake," Kellach shouted back. "I'll be there in a minute."

Driskoll turned back to Moyra. He cupped his hands around his mouth and yelled into her ear. "Wake up!"

Moyra winced. "Bugbear breath," she mumbled. "Go away."

Kellach came through the door, holding two steaming mugs.

"I thought you'd never get here," Driskoll said, nodding at the mug. "Is that a potion? Can I have some?"

"Funny. I don't recall you being bitten by a snake." Kellach knelt next to Moyra. "And anyway, you wouldn't like it. It's elven tea. Dad drinks it when he has to work long hours. Maybe it'll keep both of us awake for a while."

"Here, Moyra." Kellach held the mug up to her nose so she could smell it.

Moyra opened one eye and looked at Kellach. She took the mug and sniffed it.

She managed to open both eyes and then she took a sip. "Mmm," she smiled. "Good."

"Keep drinking," Kellach directed her.

"I wish we could give this to Dad," Driskoll said, watching Moyra's eyes open a little wider.

"I know," Kellach said, sipping the tea. "But he has to be awake. We can't just pour hot tea down a sleeping person's throat. He'd choke and suffocate."

Moyra downed the tea and smacked her lips. Her eyes were open wider, but were still a little glazed. "That was delicious," she said. "So where are we going?"

"To Zendric's," Kellach answered, finishing his tea. "How are you feeling?"

She shrugged. "Still tired. But I think I can make it."

"Can you walk?" Kellach reached out to help her up.

She wobbled to the door. "Of course I can walk," she said. "Where are we going again?"

Kellach sighed. "Zendric's," he answered, watching her walk out the front door and down the path. "And you're going the wrong way."

∎　❙　❙　❙　❙

"Finally," Driskoll said when they reached Zendric's door. It had been a long trip, between trying to explain everything to Moyra about a dozen times and Moyra leaning her head on Driskoll's shoulder as they walked.

The good thing was that trying to support her while keeping Suma hidden in his pocket had kept his mind off the Inevitable.

They pushed Moyra into Zendric's sitting room, where she immediately found a fat armchair by the fireplace and curled up in it. The boys looked around. Zendric wasn't there.

"He's probably upstairs," Kellach said. They scrambled up the wooden staircase and opened the door at the top. Inside, Zendric sat in his chair, his head resting on his ornately carved wooden desk.

"He's fallen asleep sitting up," Kellach said. They rushed over to him and Kellach gently eased the old wizard back against the chair. He brushed the long white hair from Zendric's sleeping face.

"Looks like he was trying to write something," Kellach said, turning to the scrap of parchment on the desk.

"What's it say?" a sleepy voice behind them asked. The boys turned.

"Moyra, I thought you were asleep."

She shrugged. "A little rest in Zendric's chair and I'm feeling better."

Driskoll rubbed the spot on his shoulder where her head had clunked him as they walked. "*Now* she feels better," he muttered.

"So what does that scroll say?" Moyra asked. "All I can see are scratches and blotches."

"He must have fallen asleep as he wrote," Kellach said. "His writing is all over the page." He traced his finger along the wide scribbles and shook the parchment gently. Then he waved a hand over it.

"That's better," he said. Driskoll and Moyra watched as the looping circles and crooked lines moved around the page. Slowly, they began to form and became actual letters.

Kellach read. "'Inevitable . . . Show Silver Dragon for . . . you.'"

Driskoll scratched his head. "'Show Silver Dragon for you'? That doesn't make sense."

Kellach frowned. "Not 'you,'" he said. "'Yu.' See?" He pointed to the handwriting.

Driskoll looked at the parchment. *"Y-U,"* he read. "It still doesn't make sense. I mean, Zendric can spell, can't he?"

Kellach groaned. "Of course Zendric can spell," he grumbled. "I think he was trying to write a whole word, but *Y-U* is as far as he got before he fell asleep. See how it trails off? Even the decipher charm can't help us read the rest of it."

Driskoll looked again at the sleeping wizard. "But he wrote something about the Inevitable, right?" he asked. "So Zendric knows about it. And that proves the Inevitable is the cause of this disease, not the snakes."

"It proves nothing," Kellach answered, still studying Zendric. "But it is another clue." He looked again at the parchment. "'Show Silver Dragon,'" he repeated. "I think he may have been trying to tell us something."

The old elf's head had fallen forward again. Kellach propped it up against the back of the chair, and they could see that his robes were disheveled around his neck.

"Here," Kellach said, loosening the collar. "Take a look at this." He pointed at a mark shaped like a Y on the wizard's neck.

85

Moyra studied it. "Is it a vampire bite?" she asked. "It looks familiar."

"You're right it looks familiar," Kellach answered. "You've got one too." He nodded at her left hand.

"Me?" Moyra held up her arm. "Where?"

"Right there, above your thumb," Kellach said. "It's where the snake bit you, isn't it?"

Moyra looked closely at the back of her hand, rubbing it with her other thumb. "Oh, yeah," she said. "I kind of see something . . . I think."

"What do you mean, 'kind of'?" Kellach asked, taking her hand and looking at it. "Well, that's odd."

"What?" Driskoll asked, looking over Kellach's shoulder.

"The mark," Kellach said. "The one shaped like a snake's tongue. It's faded."

"Hmm." Driskoll squinted at Moyra's hand. "But it's still there. A tiny bit of it, anyway."

Moyra pulled her hand away. "Are you two finished?" she asked.

"But it's another good sign, isn't it?" Driskoll tapped Kellach's shoulder eagerly. "Moyra's mark is gone and she's awake."

"I suppose," Kellach said.

Driskoll pushed aside Kellach's long blond hair and peeked at his brother's neck. "Have you still got your mark, Kellach?" Driskoll asked.

Kellach brushed him away. "Cut that out," he said.

But Driskoll wasn't about to be stopped. "Yep," he answered his own question. "Still there."

Kellach gave him an annoyed look and then went back to the

parchment. "This *Y-U*," he said. "It's that letter *Y* again."

"Do you think that's important?" Driskoll asked.

"Of course," Kellach answered. "Many people have a Y-shaped mark, and Zendric's note says, 'show Silver Dragon for'—something that starts with the letter *Y*."

"But Moyra's *Y* has faded," Driskoll said hopefully.

Moyra looked at the mark on Zendric's neck. "It looks familiar," she said. "I've seen it somewhere else."

"Gwinton's got one too," Kellach said. "So does my dad. And that's too many of these things for this to be a coincidence," he added, looking at Driskoll as if he knew Driskoll was about to say that.

"This isn't a random thing," he continued. "I'm guessing that Dad and Gwinton got the mark when they were at the blacksmith's shop fighting off those snakes."

Driskoll shook his head and walked to Zendric's big fireplace. He leaned against the mantel. "I still think the Inevitable is giving everyone this disease. And don't forget those dire wolves in the cathedral. They could be spreading it too."

"But Moyra wasn't bitten by a wolf," Kellach said, looking straight at him. "And neither was I. Face it, Dris. Snakes bit us. They're all over Curston, just like this disease. They're probably poisoning us with their venom. And I'm pretty sure they're leaving this mark behind—the mark of the snake's tongue—to show that it's them."

Driskoll sighed loudly and shook his head. He reached into his pocket and felt for Suma. The little snake responded by tickling his finger with its tongue. "But Suma is a good snake," he said weakly.

"Look," Kellach said. "Maybe you're right about the Inevitable. Maybe it's sending the snakes to us. I mean, it showed up at the same time as the snakes did. But I still think the snakes are giving us this mark and this disease by biting us."

"Still," Driskoll said, taking his hands out of his pockets and resting them on the mantelpiece. "You gotta admit that it's a good sign that Moyra woke up."

"I don't know," Kellach said. "The rest of the city is still asleep."

"The rest of the city?" Moyra repeated. "You mean my mother and father too?"

Kellach nodded. "We're pretty sure this has affected everyone."

"So," she ran her fingers through her red hair. "If your dad and Gwinton are asleep, and everyone in the city's asleep, then that means all the watchers are asleep too."

Kellach and Driskoll nodded.

"Then I have a question," she continued. "If everyone's asleep, who's guarding the Westgate?"

Kellach and Driskoll gaped at each other. Driskoll didn't want to think about the entire city being left open and unguarded. He didn't want to think about anything else. Neither, apparently, did Kellach. He'd already started dragging Moyra down the staircase.

"Come on, Moyra," he said. "We're going to the Westgate."

CHAPTER

13

Moyra had trouble keeping up. She leaned against Driskoll most of the way until he got tired of her shoulder bag knocking up against him, and he steered her away.

Kellach stopped and looked around. "Do you feel something?" he asked.

"Actually, no," Driskoll said, glaring at Moyra. "I can't feel my right side anymore."

"No, I mean . . . something's watching us." Kellach looked around. They were walking along a curving pathway lined with bent old oak trees that led out of the Wizards' Quarter.

Driskoll stopped. He felt in his pocket for Suma. The little snake wasn't there. He patted his hands against his jacket. "Suma!" he yelled. "Suma's missing."

Kellach said nothing. He pointed at a tall stone warehouse about ten paces ahead, where something moved along the roofline. It was large and had a pair of familiar green eyes.

"It's the same snake that was at our front door," Kellach said under his breath.

Moyra perked up and stared at the snake, but Driskoll was more interested in finding his pet.

"Suma," Driskoll whispered, looking around wildly. "Where is he?"

Moyra and Kellach ignored Driskoll and watched the snake slither down the building. Moyra gasped.

"Don't worry," Kellach reassured her. "It didn't bother us the last time we saw it."

The snake curved around the base of the old warehouse, watching them all the while. Then it slid away and disappeared into the twisted streets.

Moyra took a deep breath. "What was that all about?"

"It's strange," Kellach said. "We saw that snake earlier at our house, and it did the same thing. It just watched us and then it went away."

"Yeah, and it seems like the last time we saw that snake, Suma went missing," Driskoll said suspiciously.

Kellach frowned. "I really don't think that has anything to do with your snake, Dris," he said. "It's just a coincidence."

Driskoll glowered at his older brother while he searched the road.

"When did you notice he was gone?" Moyra asked, still looking at the spot on the building where the snake had been.

"I had him with me when we were at Zendric's. I felt him in my pocket when I was near the fireplace. Come on. Help me look for him." Driskoll started heading back along the path.

"No," Kellach said sternly. "We've got to get to the gate.

Your snake will find its way home. It's smarter than you think."

Driskoll stopped and looked Kellach in the eye. "First of all, Suma isn't an 'it,'" he said. "He's a 'he.'"

"How do you know?" Moyra asked.

"I-I just know. You two wouldn't understand."

"Why wouldn't we?" Kellach asked.

"Because neither of you understand snakes. You don't even like snakes. And if you—"

Kellach cut him off. "Come on, Driskoll. If no one's guarding the gate, anyone could get into town, and your little snake—and all of us—are in greater danger than ever."

Kellach was right. If they were the only ones in Curston who were awake, they needed to guard their city. He'd have to look for Suma later. Driskoll turned and trudged back to the street, following Kellach and Moyra. They all walked in silence while Driskoll kept his eyes open for Suma.

They crossed through the deserted and silent Main Square, and the old nagging thought came to Driskoll. This was where they had last seen the Inevitable. Suppose it was here somewhere, lurking around a corner. He reached for his poker stick.

Kellach smirked. "You planning to fight the Inevitable with that?"

"Better than nothing," Driskoll responded grimly.

They stopped in front of the ruined blacksmith's shop and looked at the piles of rubble. Driskoll spotted Grayson and his father still asleep near the elf maiden's cart.

"They look so comfortable," Moyra said. "Maybe I could stay here while you two go on."

Kellach shook his head and dragged her by the hand. "It's not much farther. You can rest later."

"Come on," Driskoll urged her. "Let's get out of here. That Inevitable could have rebuilt itself by now."

Block after silent block they walked through Main Square and into the New Quarter. Driskoll listened for that horrible clanking—he knew he'd never forget that sound as long as he lived.

But the only noise they heard was the sound of their own footsteps as they crept slowly through the city.

And then Driskoll heard it. It was faint, but it was definitely a clanking sound.

"What's that?" he asked, stopping short.

The others stopped too.

"I didn't hear anything," Moyra said.

"It could be on another street," Kellach suggested with a slight shake in his voice.

Driskoll looked around. "I don't hear it anymore," he whispered. "Let's keep moving."

They took a few more steps.

Clink.

"I don't like this," Kellach said. "It's not as loud, but we're completely exposed." He looked at the other two. "Either of you have any ideas?"

Driskoll and Moyra shook their heads, and they took a few more steps.

Clink, clink, clink.

Kellach stopped and looked at Moyra. "Do me a favor," he said. "Take a few more steps, all by yourself."

"But I'm tired . . . "

"Just do it," Kellach commanded.

Moyra sighed and took three steps.

Clink. Clink. Clink.

She looked at her side and laughed out loud. "My bag!" she snickered. "Here's your big scary monster!"

Driskoll rolled his eyes. "So your stupid bag is making all that noise?" He reached for it. "What do you carry in that thing?"

Moyra stopped laughing and clutched it close. "Get your dirty claws off it," she grumped. "It's personal."

"Come on," Kellach said. "We're all a little jumpy. It's bad enough that the whole town's falling asleep. Let's not start hearing things."

"You were just as scared as I was," Driskoll said under his breath.

"Be quiet," Kellach chided. "I can see the gate."

Driskoll squinted ahead. Where normally he could see the massive wood and iron doors of the fifty-foot-tall gate, now he could see the wide-open spaces of the world beyond. And that could mean only one thing.

"It's wide open," Kellach whispered.

Normally, watchers patrolled the gate day and night, alert as wildcats to any trickery meant to distract them from their job of keeping beasts and monsters out of Curston. Now, two watchers—a half-orc and a human—lay fast asleep near an open fire grate in the wall.

"Great," Driskoll said. "Who knows what's been coming and going through here?"

Kellach tried to rouse the watchers, but it was no good.

They slept soundly and deeply. He checked their hands and showed them to Driskoll. It was hard for Driskoll to ignore the mark shaped like the Y of a snake's tongue.

Driskoll tried to change the subject. "Well, at least we know how the Inevitable got in." He pointed at the unguarded gate.

Kellach studied the open doors. "I don't know whether it would be better to close the gate and keep any more creatures out, or leave it open to chase them out of here."

Driskoll straightened. "Kellach, what do you think Dad would do?"

Kellach sighed. "Good question. I think Dad would be worried about the safety of the city more than anything. And he'd want to protect it from anyone or anything else that might get in."

Driskoll nodded.

"So that settles it," Kellach said. "We close the gate."

"Okay." Driskoll strolled to one of the doors. "Give me a hand here." He pushed at the gate. It was surprisingly light. He gave it another push and the gigantic doors swung shut as if they were made of twigs and not heavy oak.

"Hey, Kellach," Driskoll shouted. "Did you see how easy it was for me to close the gate? It was almost like magi—"

But a look back at Kellach with his arms raised, staring in perfect concentration at the closed gate stopped him.

"Oh," he said quietly.

Kellach raised an eyebrow. "Simple spell," he muttered. He bent down and puzzled over the sleeping watchers. "I wonder why they're here near the fire grate."

"To keep warm?" Driskoll suggested.

"But it's the middle of summer," Kellach said. "They don't need a fire to keep them warm. Wait a minute." He sprang up and looked at Driskoll.

"Remember at the blacksmith's? We saw all those sweep marks. Where did they start?"

"Near the fireplace," Driskoll said, comprehension beginning to dawn on him.

"And Moyra," Kellach turned to where she'd been standing a minute earlier. "Where'd she go? Moyra?"

Driskoll sighed and pointed at Kellach's feet. Moyra had sat down on the cobblestones. She'd drawn her knees up to her chest and leaned her head on them.

"Moyra?" Kellach bent down and tapped her shoulder.

"What? I'm awake," she said, startled.

"Where were you when the snake bit you?" Kellach asked. She had to think for a moment. "I was at my house, sweeping out the fireplace."

Driskoll knelt down. "St. Cuthbert's," he said. "The snakes in there, they were right near that grate in the floor where the clerics burn their incense."

"Uh huh." Kellach nodded excitedly. "Every time we've seen a bunch of snakes, they're always near a fireplace or a fire grate."

"Well, Selik said they like warm places, right?" Driskoll said.

"Right," Kellach agreed, studying the grate in the wall. "But I don't think that's the whole reason they're near fireplaces."

He looked again at Moyra, who was following along, but just barely. "Do you know anything about this grate here?" he asked.

Moyra looked at it. "Sure," she said. "It's a tunnel. Leads into the prison. My father said it used to be an escape route until the watchers built a fireplace at this end."

"Wait a minute," Driskoll said. "The grate in the cathedral. I've heard it leads to the catacombs below the building."

"Uh huh," Kellach said. "And the fireplace at the blacksmith's been around since before the Sundering of the Seal. Who knows what that leads to."

"So what do you think, Kellach?"

"I think it's how snakes are getting into the city." He looked at Driskoll. "And one more thing. You said the last time you had your snake was at Zendric's. Do you remember where you were standing?"

Driskoll didn't like where the conversation was going. "I was at the fireplace," he said. "But it doesn't mean anything."

Kellach squinted at him. "Driskoll, you're going to have to face it sooner or later. That thing is involved with this."

Driskoll squinted back. "Suma is not a 'thing.' He's my pet. And he's not involved."

Kellach looked away. "How do you know for sure?"

Driskoll clenched his jaw. "So you think Suma is putting everyone to sleep, huh? Selik said he's just a common garden snake."

Kellach looked back at Driskoll. "What was he doing in St. Cuthbert's with all those wolves? And what did he do to Moyra back at the house?"

"I don't know," Driskoll shouted. "But I know he wouldn't hurt anyone."

"Hmpf," Kellach said under his breath. "Never trust a snake."

"I heard that," Driskoll shouted. "I'm going to look for Suma because I trust my pet." He stomped away and Kellach didn't stop him.

In a few minutes, Driskoll found himself at Watchers' Hall.

A few more watchers lay sleeping quietly near the main door. Driskoll stopped when he noticed a figure in black robes moving among the sleeping guards.

Driskoll held his breath as he watched. The figure worked silently—apparently unaware of Driskoll—as he bent down toward one of the watchers.

But Driskoll's eye was drawn to the sleeping watcher who was lounging on his back with his head resting on a rock. Something was spinning around the watcher's head. It was like thousands of tiny white stars.

The stars swirled into a colorful shape of some kind—it looked like a large red crab or spider. The next moment, the crab was blue. Then it dissolved into stars again and became a child or a dwarf; Driskoll couldn't tell. And it was purple. The colorful figure hovered in front of the watcher's face, and if Driskoll didn't know the man was sound asleep, he would have thought he was watching the figure as it changed and danced before his eyes like a colorful show.

Driskoll was fascinated. He'd never seen anything like this, except maybe in a dream.

The black-clad figure drew his attention again as he pulled something from his robes. It was a small clay pot. The figure removed the lid and held the base of the pot underneath the swirling stars.

Driskoll suddenly realized that the figure's robes looked a lot like those of the clerics from the cathedral. He breathed a sigh of relief as he ran toward the figure.

"Thank the gods," Driskoll said. "We thought all the clerics were sick. Now you can help cure everyone."

The cleric stood up, quickly clamping the cover down on the pot. The stars dissolved into the air.

The cleric's face remained hidden, but Driskoll barely noticed. A large black snake was slithering around the cleric's feet.

"Watch out," Driskoll yelled. The cleric disappeared. All Driskoll could see was the snake. Its large black eyes watched him carefully as it swept toward him.

Driskoll wondered if he was dreaming, because he couldn't seem to move. The snake came closer and Driskoll saw that it was the biggest one he had ever seen. He could see a huge gaping mouth, like a dark, black tunnel. But still, he couldn't move.

Glistening white fangs guarded the tunnel and grew closer every moment. Driskoll could see into it—it seemed to lead into a void of black space. A voice was telling him that Moyra, Kellach, and Suma were deep inside the tunnel, and he had to go inside to get them out. He moved forward into the tunnel, toward those fangs . . .

Then two gigantic needles pierced his head as the teeth closed on him. At the same moment, a powerful blow hit the back of his skull and sent him flying. There was another blow as his head struck something solid.

And then everything went black.

CHAPTER

14

Driskoll awoke to late afternoon sunlight and a stinging, burning feeling on his forehead. But more than that, he was confused. The giant snake had been coming at him from the front, but the blow had come from behind him.

He looked around. The snake was gone. The cleric was gone. Kellach was standing over him, glaring angrily. Moyra leaned against Kellach, her eyes half closed.

"Why did you wander off?" Kellach demanded. "That snake bit you."

"I know," Driskoll said. "But something hit me in the back of the head too."

"Yeah," Kellach said, reaching out to help Driskoll up. "You were leaning toward it like you were going to kiss it or something. I yelled but you didn't do anything. So I threw that spell to knock you away. Then you landed on that hard head of yours."

"I think . . . I think it hypnotized me," Driskoll said. "I just couldn't move." He reached up and felt his forehead.

Kellach gaped at him. "Looks like I was too late," he said. "You've been bitten. And you've got a mark—just next to your eye."

"Funny the snakebite doesn't hurt nearly as much as what you did," Driskoll grumped, rubbing the back of his head.

"That's not half as bad as how you're going to feel when you fall asleep forever," Kellach said.

"Wait." Driskoll looked around. "Maybe the cleric can help me."

"What cleric?" Kellach stopped and followed Driskoll's eyes as he glanced around.

"Didn't either of you see him?" Driskoll looked from Moyra to Kellach.

They shook their heads. Driskoll pointed at the sleeping watcher. "He was right there."

"The clerics are all sick, Dris," Kellach said quietly. "Are you sure you weren't dreaming?"

"I was dreaming at some point," he answered. "But I wasn't dreaming when I saw the cleric. He was standing right there."

Moyra blinked. "You're really confusing me, Driskoll," she said.

Kellach walked over to the sleeping watcher and picked something up off the ground. He held it up.

"That's it!" Driskoll yelled. "That's the clay pot. The cleric was holding it. It had a lid. And—and there were stars."

Kellach looked puzzled. "Stars?"

"Yeah," Driskoll said. "Like a rainbow, only . . . not. They turned into a crab or a spider or something."

Kellach frowned. "I'm worried about you," he said.

"Just open up the pot," Driskoll said. "I think the cleric was using whatever was in there to help the watcher."

Kellach shot a skeptical look at Driskoll before he removed the lid and looked inside. "Empty," he said.

Driskoll sighed. "But that's the pot. The cleric was holding it. I think he was curing that watcher."

Kellach looked at the sleeping watcher. "He doesn't look any better," he said, shaking his head. "Who was the cleric?"

"Dunno," Driskoll said. "I've never seen him before."

Kellach raised an eyebrow. "Well, where is he now?"

Driskoll tried to remember. "I don't know where he went. He was there one minute, and then the snake came and he was gone. He must have been frightened and he ran away from it."

Kellach nodded. "Sensible thing to do," he said. "Wish you'd thought of that."

Driskoll shrugged. "I just couldn't move."

Kellach examined the pot. "It's exactly like the ones Selik gave you," he said. "You know, maybe these pots do somehow have healing power. Maybe they're an antidote to this illness."

"We should go to Selik's and find out." Driskoll yawned.

"That's a good idea," Moyra added. "You two go to Selik's and I'll go home and take a little nap." She began to walk away, but Kellach grabbed her by the shoulder.

"Sorry," he said. "You're staying with us. I don't want that Inevitable chasing after you in your condition."

"But we should hurry," Driskoll said. "There's no telling how much time we have before we're all asleep."

▮ ▮ ▮ ▮ ▮

It was a much slower walk to Broken Town, and Driskoll was starting to feel sleepy.

But he was rattled. Now that he himself had been struck—and in such a strange way, as if he'd been hypnotized—he couldn't deny that snakes were the ones who were putting everyone to sleep.

And like Kellach had said, this wasn't random. Someone or something was doing this on purpose. Maybe it was the Inevitable, but to Driskoll, the more important question right now was whether Suma had anything to do with it.

Driskoll couldn't see how his little pet could be involved. But Kellach's questions nagged at him. What had Suma been doing in St. Cuthbert's with those wolves? Why had he been crawling over Moyra today? Who had smashed those clay pots? And where was Suma now?

Driskoll imagined Suma crawling down through Zendric's chimney to a meeting place below the city where other snakes had gathered.

I've got to stop this, he thought. I'm getting sleepy and now I'm imagining all sort of strange things.

Moyra had been leaning her head on his shoulder for several minutes.

"How does she do it?" Driskoll asked, pushing her gently over to Kellach's shoulder. "How can she be sleeping and walking at the same time?"

"I'm not sleeping," Moyra said, her head bouncing on Kellach's shoulder as he walked beside her. "I'm resting. I'll get my energy back in a minute. That tea ought to kick in again soon."

Driskoll didn't even try to understand her logic. She was overly tired and he was sleepy too.

"Moyra, it's bad enough that you're using my shoulder as a pillow, but could you get rid of whatever is in your bag? It feels like you're carrying a rock in there."

Moyra looked up at him sleepily. Her eyes widened a bit. "Of course," she said. "My bag. The book!" She rummaged around her bag and pulled out the book she had lifted from Selik's shop.

She held it up.

Driskoll stared blankly at it. The book's jewel-encrusted cover shone brightly in the afternoon light, but the gold embossed Y in the center of the book cover stood out even more.

Kellach stared at the book. "It's exactly like the mark that we have."

Moyra nodded. "I knew I had seen this mark before." She held the book out to Kellach, who took it and began flipping through it. Driskoll looked over his brother's shoulder. Most of the pages were blank, but the first few pages were lined with handwriting.

"Looks like a journal," Kellach said. "But it's in another language. I think I can decipher it, but"—he rubbed his eyes—"I'm really tired."

Kellach handed the book back to her. "Hang on to this," he said. "Maybe we can figure it out later. In the meantime, let's keep heading for Selik's. I think he's got an antidote that can help us."

They passed the Skinned Cat, where a hairless panther stared boldly at them from the dangling, faded sign.

"That panther's the only thing in Broken Town with its eyes open," Driskoll observed as they slipped past it.

Everything about the Skinned Cat looked the same. It smelled the same too, Driskoll thought, wrinkling his nose. But one thing was different. The usual riot of sound from the tavern was gone.

They continued walking until they reached the empty store-front Moyra had shown them earlier. They slipped into the dark space between the buildings and came around to the back.

"I'll sit down here," Moyra said, leaning against the dragon-covered wall. "You two go ahead."

"No, Moyra." Kellach shook his head.

"I'll be a lookout," she offered as her back slid down the wall and she landed on the ground.

"You won't be looking out for anything. You'll just take a nap."

But Moyra's head had fallen forward. She was already asleep.

"Maybe I can sit with her for a minute," Driskoll suggested, drifting toward her. But Kellach pulled him toward the back of the yard. "Come on. We've got to find that door."

Driskoll groaned. "The last thing I want to do right now is deal with that stupid dragon painting."

"Yeah, well, it'll be the last thing you do if we don't find some sort of cure, and Selik's our only hope at the moment," Kellach said.

Driskoll looked at his brother. Kellach's eyes were red and his lids were half closed. His usual tan skin had a gray tinge, and his long blond hair hung limply.

Just knowing that Kellach was tired but still determined gave Driskoll a little more energy. He looked up at the dragon. "All right, you," he growled. "Where's your stupid door?"

The dragon winked at him.

Getting into the dragon's door should have been easier now that Driskoll already knew the pattern of the disappearing door. But he was slower now, and as he ran for the door in the place where he expected it to be, it began to fade. With one last bit of energy, he sprinted forward and into the darkness.

"Whew," he panted, as he realized he'd made it inside. He nearly doubled over from exhaustion, but Kellach was behind him in only a few seconds, supporting him.

Inside, they heard voices coming from Selik's rooms below. They stole quietly down the ramp and listened outside. One of the voices belonged to Selik. The other was a boy. They were arguing loudly. Kellach peered inside the shop and motioned to Driskoll. Driskoll followed Kellach inside. Selik and the boy must have been in a room beyond.

It was darker than Driskoll remembered it, and the dragon fireplace had gone out again. Driskoll looked around the walls. The corner where the pots had been now stood empty. All of the clay pots that had been stacked against the wall were gone, leaving the wall painting exposed. The boys stared at it.

The painting showed a boy—a human boy—kneeling before a giant black snake. The boy held up a clay pot, and a stream of stars seemed to be lifting out of the pot toward the snake. Driskoll tapped Kellach on the shoulder and pointed at the painting.

Kellach nodded, but he seemed more interested in the voices from the other room.

"You have stolen what does not belong to you," Selik shouted.

"No, you've taken them," the younger voice replied. "I'm just returning everything to the owners. And I could have returned them to the girl if you hadn't shown up."

As they listened, Kellach sleepily traced the outline of the colors in the painting. His finger made a scratching sound and the voices stopped.

Driskoll heard a swishing sort of noise. "Where are you going?" Selik snapped. "Come back here."

A moment later he huffed through the doorway in the middle of one of the paintings. Selik's eyes were narrow and he was frowning.

"Sorry you had to hear that, lads," he said. "Uh, how much did you hear?"

"Nothing much," Driskoll said. "But who were you talking to?"

"Ah, that's not important," Selik waved his hand airily. "I'll bet you're here because you've been bitten."

"Yeah, how did you know?" Driskoll asked.

"I know that mark well," Selik explained, pointing at Driskoll's forehead.

"We thought you might have a cure," Kellach said.

"A cure?" Selik smiled.

"Yeah, we thought maybe it has something to do with those pots that were stacked against the wall." Driskoll explained.

Selik looked at the wall where the pots had been. "Ah, the pots," he said. "Yes. They are performing their function right now. But I do have two more here that I've saved just for you."

He picked up two pots from a dusty table on the edge of the room.

"So they are a cure?" Kellach asked.

"A cure? Well, let's just put it this way," Selik answered. "I don't think your father would approve."

"Why not?" Kellach asked. "Is the cure somehow illegal?"

"To the feeble minded it is illegal," Selik answered. "But to those with a higher intelligence, these simple clay pots can transform."

"But they're illegal," Kellach said, "whatever they are. And if they're illegal, there's probably a good reason. They're probably dangerous or something."

"My dear boy," Selik said, taking a step forward with the two pots. "Do you want me to help you or not?"

"Well, of course we do, but . . . "

He held a pot in each hand and gazed at the boys. Driskoll suddenly felt uncomfortable as Selik took another step toward them, holding the pots.

"All right," Kellach said. "What's in those pots?"

But a deafening crash outside interrupted everything.

Kellach and Driskoll looked around frantically. There was a huge blast and the building shook around them.

"What in the name of holy dragons is that?" Selik shrieked, dropping the clay pots on the floor.

Kellach and Driskoll turned around just as a huge golden statue with menacing eyes charged through the archway.

CHAPTER

15

Chunks of stone and brick rained down. The Inevitable's golden eyes swiveled in their sockets as it searched for its prey. Driskoll saw a flash of silver in the Inevitable's hand.

"My sword!" Driskoll yelled.

There it was, the thing he valued most in the world besides Suma. And now it was in the hands of this murdering, destructive giant.

Driskoll felt a fury he had never known before. He couldn't think of anything else except his sword. The Inevitable's eyes had latched onto him and it was staring at Driskoll with what looked like a burning desire to destroy.

He could hear the clank of the Inevitable's huge body as it charged forward, and he watched as it toppled the dragon fireplace as if it were a child's toy. He could hear the cold, mechanical voice, but he didn't care. He was far angrier than he was afraid.

The Inevitable didn't seem to notice as Selik edged along the wall around them, disappearing through the huge, blown-out hole that used to be the stone archway.

Both boys backed up toward the wall. Driskoll knew they had no way of escaping like Selik had done. The Inevitable wanted them, and as proof, it carried Driskoll's sword.

"Any ideas?" Kellach yelled over the clanking.

Driskoll fingered the poker stick he had picked up in the blacksmith's forge. He had been keeping it in the hilt where he normally kept his sword. He watched as the creature banged toward him. That alabaster armor was impossible to penetrate. The little metal rod was useless.

"Unless . . . " Driskoll held the poker stick up.

"What are you doing?" Kellach yelled.

Driskoll steadied himself. It was a crazy idea, but it was all they had left.

"Come and get me," he whispered hoarsely, narrowing his eyes at the creature. But he wasn't looking at its inhuman eyes. He focused on its knees.

The creature lurched forward. Closer, closer, it thrashed like an oversized mad pony, and its legs were a blur of movement. It would be next to impossible to get the poker exactly where Driskoll wanted it.

The creature continued walking forward, its chain whipping the air.

Driskoll stood his ground. The creature took one final, clanking step closer. It was only inches from him. Driskoll jammed the poker into the Inevitable's knee.

The Inevitable reared up and then came down hard. Driskoll and Kellach were just under its body, between its legs, which were thrashing around them like wild maces.

Driskoll braced for a killer kick from those powerful legs. But it never came.

The poker stick wedged into its knee had stopped a single gear, and it had been enough.

The Inevitable repeated its droning mechanical phrase one last time and then crumpled to the ground. The boys dodged the falling metal, and Driskoll surveyed the pile of golden spokes and gears, looking for his sword. It had to be buried in there somewhere. But how was he going to get it out?

An open eye stared back up at him from the pile of golden gears.

"Come on, Driskoll," Kellach whispered. "We have to check on Moyra."

Neither of them wanted to say what they were thinking—that Moyra was sitting outside when the Inevitable crashed through the building. Had she survived?

Driskoll knew he had to check on Moyra, but he couldn't help thinking about his sword. He took one more look at the pile of gadgets and gears, but he couldn't see his trusty weapon anywhere. "Dragon dung," he swore.

"You can get it later," Kellach whispered.

Driskoll kicked a gear across the room and followed Kellach. The boys raced up the hallway, which had brightened considerably since the Inevitable had torn down the walls. Most of it was exposed now to the outside air.

Breathing hard, they jumped out the opening in the wall and looked around the littered yard.

Moyra was gone.

CHAPTER

16

W here is she?" Driskoll yelled.

Kellach bent down to pick up something from the ground. "Moyra's shoulder bag," he said, picking it up.

"Come on, Kellach. We didn't have time to look for my sword, let's not waste any more time. We have to find Moyra."

Kellach nodded and slung the bag over his shoulder. It was growing dark now. Normally curfew would begin in a few minutes, and the streets would be empty. But there were no watchers to ring the bells at St. Cuthbert's and announce the beginning of the restriction.

They headed toward the edge of Broken Town. Driskoll was starting to get used to the ghostly quiet of the empty city, which was why he stopped and gasped when they rounded the corner of the Skinned Cat.

The street was full of people.

"Hey, they're awake," Driskoll said as a crowd of about twenty or thirty people headed toward them.

Driskoll didn't know many people from Broken Town beyond Moyra, her family, and a few others. But he could tell by the ragged clothes and skinny, half-starved bodies that these people were from the poorest section of Curston.

Each one of them carried a small clay pot with a lid. They held the pots out in front of them with both hands as if they were bearing gifts. But there was something else. There was something very different about these people. Driskoll couldn't put his finger on it.

"Look, it's Moyra's mom," Kellach called out.

Driskoll could see a woman shuffling at the edge of the crowd. He could tell by the shock of red hair—the same color as Moyra's—that it was indeed Moyra's mom, Royma. But that was the only way he could tell. Royma's eyes looked dazed and unfocused, and her sunken cheeks were as gray as the pebbles on the street. She had the stiff-legged, dragging gait of a zombie.

And that's when Driskoll realized what was so different. None of these people looked human anymore.

"Great gods," Driskoll whispered, grabbing Kellach's arm. "They're like zombies."

"But I think they're all asleep," Kellach said. "And where is Moyra?"

Driskoll didn't have time to answer. The front door of the Skinned Cat flew open and another crowd of people streamed through it, joining the larger group in the street. Driskoll saw Patch, the deformed but kindly old elf and barkeeper. There were other creatures too—half-orcs, elves, humans—all of the others who spent their days at the Skinned Cat.

Driskoll and Kellach backed up to the wall of the tavern as the crowd flowed past them.

"Where are they going?" Driskoll wondered aloud.

"Let's just follow them," Kellach said. "Maybe we'll find Moyra."

The boys edged along the side of the moving mob, looking for a sign of Moyra's telltale red hair.

"Do you see her anywhere?" Kellach called.

Driskoll shook his head. He was fighting a growing desire to settle down on the side of the road and close his eyes. The fight with the Inevitable seemed to have stolen what little energy he'd had left.

"Seems like they're heading toward the Westgate," Kellach called back. "Good thing we closed it."

Driskoll didn't answer. He had to save his energy. He kept pace with the crowd and soon they were at the Westgate.

A small clutch of people was already there, and from the looks of it, the townsfolk were from Main Square and other areas of Curston. They all stood silently at the great doors, staring straight ahead, silent as corpses. Driskoll looked around.

"Grayson," he called, moving forward.

The blacksmith's son hadn't heard Driskoll. He just stood along with the others in the crowd, staring straight ahead.

Grayson didn't even seem to be aware of his father standing near him. No one showed any signs that they were even alive, except that they were breathing very softly.

"Moyra's not here," Kellach said as he came up beside Driskoll. "Let's go home and see if we can find her . . . and Dad."

"Yeah," Driskoll answered blankly, still staring at the haunting faces of Grayson and his dad. There was something almost frightening about the way everyone stood at the door, as if they were waiting for something. But the Westgate was shut and bolted tight—he and Kellach had seen to that. Driskoll didn't think any of these people were capable of opening the giant gate in their current condition.

At least he knew they couldn't let anyone in or out.

He turned and followed Kellach home.

CHAPTER

17

Where the streets of Curston had been empty before, now they were like rivers flowing with people. Driskoll had to hold on tight to Kellach as they fought their way through the strong current of crowds.

It seemed as if the entire town of Curston was heading for the Westgate. Everyone moved in the same stiff manner, and getting past them was more tiring than Driskoll could have imagined.

Kellach was beside himself. "This doesn't fit," he shouted. "I thought the snakes were biting us, and their venom was making us fall asleep. But now, I don't get what's happening at all."

"They're all turning into . . . into zombies," Driskoll said weakly.

"That's impossible," Kellach moaned. "I don't know what's going on, but I know snakes can't turn everyone into zombies."

Driskoll was exhausted, and he felt every step he took. It was like dragging his legs through cement. He knew he couldn't make it much farther, and he didn't really care what Kellach was saying.

He didn't even care if he turned into a zombie himself.

Once they were on their own street, the crowd thinned to a few stragglers. The boys stood by as Sergeant Gwinton hobbled along carrying a clay pot, completely oblivious to everything around him. And then another figure approached—a tall, burly man in the dark uniform of the captain of the watch.

"Dad!" Driskoll yelled. He forgot how tired he was and he let go of Kellach. He raced toward his father. "Dad!" he called again. Kellach ran after him, but Driskoll reached Torin first.

Driskoll grabbed Torin's arm, but it felt stiff and heavy like that of a corpse. Driskoll drew his hand away just as he saw his father's slack face with its open but unseeing eyes. Torin continued carrying his clay pot and walking. He didn't—or couldn't—see his sons walking next to him.

Another arm pulled Driskoll back toward the side of the road. "There's no point trying to talk to him," Kellach said. "He's asleep."

"But we've got to stop him," Driskoll cried. "It's Dad!"

"I know," Kellach said. "But we don't know why he's behaving this way, and we need to stop for a second and figure it all out. That's the only way we can help him."

"So what do we do?" Driskoll asked. "There's nothing left." Exhausted and hungry, he was too tired to think anymore. He just wanted to close his eyes and go to sleep right there on the ground in the middle of the street.

He felt Kellach dragging him home, felt the door opening. He could see the fireplace and the hearth in front of him.

But Kellach didn't stop at the fireplace. Instead, he dragged Driskoll into the kitchen and sat him down at the table.

"Try to stay awake for just a minute," Kellach said.

"Mmpfh?" Driskoll answered. He was vaguely aware of Kellach working behind him at the basin.

The next thing he knew, Kellach was holding a mug of steaming brown liquid up to his face. "Drink it," Kellach said. "It'll make you feel better."

Driskoll had a vague memory of Moyra sipping something warm and delicious that Kellach had made earlier. He took a sip.

"Blech!" Driskoll spat the stuff out. "It tastes like . . . like trees."

Kellach frowned guiltily. "Well, it is, sort of," he said.

"I'm drinking wood?" Driskoll put down the mug. "Is this the same stuff you gave Moyra?"

"Um, not exactly." Kellach looked a little uncomfortable. "I think I might have gotten the proportions wrong on her potion—"

"Potion?! This isn't going to make me sick, is it?"

"Come on," Kellach coaxed him "I'm sure I've got it right this time. Just drink it and you'll feel better. The effects will last longer too. And then we can go find Dad and Moyra."

Driskoll felt like dropping the mug on the floor and falling asleep right there. But the thought of his father's slack face made him take another sip. The stuff tasted terrible. "Mmm, delicious," he said sarcastically.

Kellach ignored the criticism as he, too, sipped from a mug. "See? You're feeling better already," he said cheerily. "Drink up."

"So shouldn't we get back to the Westgate to check on everyone?" Driskoll suddenly felt impatient to be moving.

"And what will we do when we get there?" Kellach snapped.

"We're no closer to solving this than we were this morning. And Dad and the others aren't going anywhere. The Westgate is locked tight."

Driskoll took a few more uneasy sips of tea and squirmed in his chair. "Kellach," he said. "Are you sure this stuff is safe to drink? I feel . . . weird. I'm still really tired and my hands are shaking."

"Well, stay awake long enough to help me figure out what to do," Kellach answered. "Why is everyone in the city waking up?"

"I wouldn't call that waking up," Driskoll said. "Everyone looked worse than when they were sleeping."

"That's what I don't get," Kellach said. "Snakes can't be poisoning everyone to turn them into zombies."

"I don't know what's going on," Driskoll said, "but I sure don't want to turn into a zombie. Did you notice if anyone still had the *Y* mark on them?"

Kellach shook his head. "Couldn't see." He stared at Moyra's shoulder bag, which he'd left on the table. "Wait a minute," he said.

Kellach rummaged through the bag and pulled out the book she'd stolen from Selik.

"Maybe there's an answer in here," he said excitedly.

"Kellach," Driskoll moaned. "I know you think books always have the answers, but this is one time—"

"There's that letter *Y*," Kellach interrupted, pointing at the cover. He opened it to the first page. "It *is* a journal. I knew it. But it's a really strange language. It's going to be difficult to translate."

"Useless book," Driskoll muttered, staring at Kellach as he studied the page intently. "Come on, Kellach. Can't you hurry it up?"

Kellach began reading out loud. "' . . . Soon the Yuan-ti shall seize the human dreams for Fosh. And we shall be great once again.'" Kellach shook his head. "Listen, Dris. 'Yuan-ti.' What letter does that start with?"

Driskoll's hand fell away from his forehead as he remembered the blood red mark on his head, and the marks on his father, Kellach, and Moyra. "Yuan-ti," he said. "It starts with the letter *Y*."

18

The boys stared at each other. "So that's what this *Y* business is all about," Driskoll said. "It's the Yuan-ti."

"Of course," Kellach said. "The Yuan-ti."

"What's the Yuan-ti?" Driskoll asked.

Kellach didn't answer. He turned a page in the book.

Driskoll cocked his head and grinned. "Hah! About time we found something Mr. Know-It-All doesn't know about." Driskoll sat back in his chair and smirked.

Kellach eyed him coldly. "'Mr. Know-It-All'? That's the best you've got?"

Driskoll shrugged. "Well, I'm very tired, in case you haven't noticed. And I was so shocked by the fact that you didn't know something that I had to put all of my energy into keeping a straight face."

Kellach rolled his eyes. "Why don't you put your energy into the problem at hand? Or were you so shocked that you forgot about Dad and Moyra?"

"I haven't forgotten," Driskoll shot back, rapping his knuckles on the book in front of them. "Read it again."

"You mean this useless book?"

"Come on, Kellach. You said we don't have time for this."

Kellach sighed. "You're right, we don't." He read again. "'Soon the Yuan-ti shall seize the human dreams for Fosh. And we shall be great once again.'" He looked up. "That's about all it says."

Driskoll shot up. "Fosh!" he yelled. "I've never heard of Yuan-ti, but I've heard of Fosh. Remember at Selik's? It was written on the painting. It said, 'To Selik, on your birthday. From Fosh.' I can't forget that because Selik said Fosh was like the father of all snake keepers."

"You're right," Kellach answered. "I remember."

"And Yuan-ti," Driskoll continued, sitting down again. "I wonder if they're snake keepers of some kind. And Fosh is their ruler."

Kellach glanced back at the book. "I suspect they're more than just snake keepers."

"What do you mean?" Driskoll asked.

"Listen to this." Kellach leaned back in his chair. "'The Yuan-ti shall seize the human dreams,'" he repeated.

"Well, that's just plain weird," Driskoll said, frowning. "How can you seize dreams? You fall asleep and dreams just . . . happen, right?"

"Of course," Kellach said. "And if everyone in town is falling asleep . . . wait a minute, Driskoll. Remember that cleric you saw near Watchers' Hall? What did you see? What was he doing?"

"He was holding the clay pot up to the watcher. And there were stars, just like in the painting at Selik's."

"Where were the stars?"

"They were swirling around the watcher's head. But they weren't just stars. They formed all different kinds of shapes."

"Like what?"

Driskoll licked the back of his hand absently. "There was a spider or something. And a dwarf, I think. But they weren't real. More like shadows."

"And the watcher was asleep, right?"

"Yeah, just like everyone else. What's your point?"

"My point is . . . " Kellach said, looking around. "My point is that when I fall asleep, what's the first thing I do?"

"You? That's easy. You snore. Loudly."

"Besides that."

"You dream."

"Exactly. Everyone dreams, right? And what do dreams look like?"

"Well, when I dream, everything's kind of . . . one minute things are real and the next they aren't. Like that spider."

Driskoll stood up. "I get it. That watcher was sleeping and having a dream. And I could see it."

Kellach nodded. "And what did the cleric do with that dream?"

"He . . . I don't know. I think he was trying to capture it in the pot."

"He seized it, right? I bet that's how they're doing it. They're somehow using magic to draw the dreams out of people's minds, and then they're putting the dreams in those pots. I knew there was something magical about those pots."

"But when you opened the pot later, there wasn't anything in there. What happened to the dream?"

"Good question," Kellach replied.

"I think I surprised him, and the dream didn't make it into the pot because it sort of faded away. Or maybe the snake surprised him. It just appeared out of nowhere and the cleric was gone."

"Hmm," Kellach mused. "And have you ever seen the cleric before?"

"Come to think of it, no." Driskoll sat down again. "I never saw his face."

"So this cleric disappeared when the snake showed up," Kellach muttered to himself. "Interesting." He looked around. "Speaking of snakes, where's yours?"

"I don't know." Driskoll got up and spent a few minutes searching the kitchen for Suma while Kellach thought.

"So," Kellach said finally. "That cleric was probably one of these Yuan-ti people. Maybe he's taking the dreams for Fosh. And I bet that's what Selik meant when he said the clay pots would transform the city. They've turned us into a bunch of zombies."

"But why?" Driskoll frowned, searching under the table. "Why would anyone want to do that?"

"It is pretty strange," Kellach agreed. "We've seen people steal all sorts of things, but never dreams."

Driskoll emerged from beneath the table. "Well, if that's all it is—a few dreams—maybe we've got nothing to worry about. They'll take some of our dreams, we'll wake up, and they'll go away. Maybe it's not a big deal."

"It's not that simple, Dris." Kellach frowned. "If someone can figure out how to tap into your brain and get something out of it when you're sleeping, that means they could control you. And these Yuan-ti are doing this to everyone in the city."

Driskoll shivered. "Okay, but what are we going to do about it? If we don't figure out something fast, we're both going to be in dreamland soon too."

"And I have a nasty feeling that once your dreams get stolen, you're not going to wake up from dreamland."

"So Dad and everyone else—"

Kellach nodded grimly.

"But we have to do something!" Driskoll shouted. "They can't just steal our dreams and get away with it."

"Hold on," Kellach said. "We still have some things to sort out. Remember in Selik's shop? He was arguing with someone about stealing."

Driskoll trudged back to his chair and flopped down. "Yeah, I remember." He sighed. "Kellach, I don't feel very—"

"That voice talking to Selik," Kellach interrupted. "I know I've heard it somewhere else."

"Me too," Driskoll agreed, holding his hands up to his face and studying them. "Weren't they talking about a girl? The only girl we know is Moyra."

"Well, Moyra did wake up," Kellach reasoned. "Maybe that's what they were talking about—" He stopped and stared at Driskoll for a long moment. "I think I know who was talking to Selik."

Suddenly there was a knock at the front door.

Driskoll jumped and looked up at Kellach. "Should we answer it?" He tried to hide the quaver in his voice.

Kellach stood up. "Well, at least we know it's not the Inevitable. That thing doesn't knock."

The knocking sounded again, harder and more insistent.

Kellach turned and headed for the sitting room. Driskoll swallowed hard and followed.

"Come on, Driskoll," a boy's voice called from outside. Driskoll stopped in his tracks halfway to the door and looked at Kellach. The voice sounded familiar. "Open up," it demanded. "It's important."

Driskoll felt the spot where his sword had been. There was nothing there now but air. He had no weapon. But he had to know who was outside. Slowly, Driskoll moved toward the door. He put his hand on the doorknob as the pounding outside continued.

Kellach stood across from him on the other side of the doorframe, breathing hard. Driskoll could feel Kellach's eyes on his hands as he slowly turned the doorknob. The door clicked and the pounding stopped. The voice outside fell silent.

Driskoll took a deep breath and cracked the door open. All he could see outside was darkness. He opened the door a bit wider, peering hard into the black night.

And then he saw it—a figure standing on the stoop in front of him. Driskoll could see teeth gleaming in the darkness.

Driskoll heard the *ffflip* of a torch being lit behind him and realized that Kellach had created a small light source. Now he could see the figure a little more clearly.

It was a boy about Driskoll's height, and he was grinning at Driskoll in an almost goofy way.

Driskoll had never seen the boy in town before, but he looked strangely familiar with his large green eyes and tattoos on his face. Driskoll stared for what seemed like several minutes before he heard Kellach's voice behind him.

"Don't let him in," Kellach growled.

"Why not?" Driskoll asked, his eyes still fixed on the stranger.

"Because," Kellach said, "that boy is Suma."

19

"So how did you know it was me?" The boy turned to Kellach, who still stood scowling in the doorway.

Kellach held the torch up to Suma. He was about Driskoll's height and thin like Driskoll, but more muscular. He wore a bright green cloak that glowed in the darkness, but it wasn't like any material Driskoll had ever seen. It was shimmery and scaly, like snakeskin.

"There were lots of clues," Kellach said in a low, accusing voice. "But I first had an idea when I saw those paintings at Selik's. There were snakes, humans, and another kind of creature that was more like a human, but with eyes like yours. So I knew there was some other kind of creature around, something that could do human stuff like smash clay pots."

"Highly intelligent," the boy nodded enthusiastically. "You would do well as a Yuan-ti."

Kellach ignored the compliment and looked at Driskoll. "But it wasn't until I heard the arguing at Selik's that I realized

it was your snake. He's spoken to us before."

Driskoll stared at Kellach and said nothing.

"Remember, Dris? In the cathedral?" Kellach asked.

Driskoll remembered the voice he had heard crying out for help. He looked at the boy, who was still nodding his head. But he looked frightened now.

"That was scariest thing that's ever happened to me," Suma said. "I couldn't even move. I have no idea how I managed to ask you for help."

"And then later on, I could sense only snake in you," Kellach continued. "Because you're a snake, through and through. But I'm guessing you've got human blood too."

Suma turned back to Driskoll. "I'm a Yuan-ti," he explained. "We're descended from people and snakes who mixed their bloodlines. I may be taking my human form right now, but at heart, I'm a cold-blooded reptile." He grinned at Kellach, who scowled back at him.

"And I was able to block you from finding out anything else about me. Yuan-ti magic is very, very strong. And I did smash those dumb pots."

Driskoll's mind was reeling with questions. "I still don't get how you figured it out, Kellach."

"Well," Kellach said in a low voice. "When you told me about the cleric at Watchers' Hall and how he disappeared when the snake showed up, that was when I knew for sure."

"I still don't understand," Driskoll said.

"The cleric didn't run away," Kellach said. "He turned into a snake."

"Still, Kellach, I don't see how you'd—"

"And we've been seeing that snake that looked so familiar," Kellach interrupted. "That helped me too. Remember he was brown with black markings? Once I figured out that there was a third kind of creature—something in between a snake and a human—I realized that the snake we were seeing was familiar not because it looked like another snake, but because it looked like a human. Who do we know who's really tan and has black tattoos all over his face? And who likes snakes?"

Driskoll tore his gaze away from Suma to think for a moment. "Selik," he said. "Of course."

Suma shivered. "Don't say his name. I try to spend as little time as possible with that one."

Driskoll shot a knowing glance at Kellach. "That's why Suma's been running away every time that big brown snake shows up. He doesn't like him."

"Yeah," Suma said. "Selik's the one who sent those dire wolves after me in the first place."

"But why?" Driskoll asked.

Suma sighed. "You know, I would love to explain all this to you, but we don't have much time."

Driskoll must have looked even more confused than he'd been for the past five minutes.

"Okay." Suma looked hard at Driskoll as if he were willing him to understand. "I know that you two and your friend Moyra saved me. All of my brothers and sisters abandoned me with the wolves in the cathedral. But you three came back. That's why I'm here. I owe you—"

"This is all very heartwarming," Kellach interrupted. "But Selik said you stole something. It's our dreams, isn't it? That's why everyone's being put to sleep. And what did you do to Moyra? Where is she?"

Suma turned and looked Kellach full in the face. "I didn't steal anything from you. And Moyra is the reason I'm here. Yeah, that was me arguing with Selik a little while ago. He thought I left, but I stuck around when I saw you. I also saw Selik sneak out when the Inevitable came in. He took your friend Moyra with him. He's bringing her to Fosh right now. And believe me, that is not good."

Kellach made a clicking noise with his teeth, and Driskoll knew he didn't believe Suma. But Suma ignored Kellach as he looked at the scar next to Driskoll's eye. He uttered a strange syllable that had to be another language. And the way he shook his head made Driskoll think Suma was swearing an oath.

"You've got the mark," Suma said. He held a hand up to Driskoll's head. "Don't move." Driskoll stared at him.

Suddenly Kellach reached out of the doorway toward Suma. "What in the name of sorcery are you doing?" Kellach shouted.

Driskoll stared helplessly as Suma grabbed Kellach around the shoulders with one long arm and moved him back into the doorway as easily and as gently as if he were moving a child out of the way of danger. Suma kept his eyes focused on Driskoll the whole time.

Out of the corner of his eye, Driskoll could see Kellach raising one arm in a spell, but he didn't see anything magical happening.

Suma stopped staring at Driskoll. "That's better." He took a deep breath and turned to Kellach. "Now you," he said.

"What did you just do to my brother?" Kellach shouted.

Driskoll couldn't help noticing that he suddenly felt much better. The jittery feeling was still there but he wasn't tired at all. He felt refreshed and wide awake, as if he'd just awakened from a deep, healthy sleep.

Suma grinned again. "I removed the mark," he said. "See?" He reached for Driskoll, but Kellach was faster. He landed a swift punch to Suma's jaw, knocking him off the stoop and onto the ground.

"Kellach! What did you do?" Driskoll shouted, jumping down to where Suma lay sprawled. But Suma sprang back up in a second.

"Didn't see that one coming," he chuckled, wiping blood from his lip.

"Don't you ever touch my brother again," Kellach said between clenched teeth.

Suma still held his hand to his lip, but he smiled. "Okay," he said. "Why don't you look for yourself, then?" He nodded at Driskoll.

Kellach held up the torch so he could see Driskoll's face, but he turned back to Suma.

"Okay, so the mark is gone. But I don't know what you did to him, and until I know more about this magic, you're not doing it to me."

"Suit yourself." Suma shrugged. "I was almost able to remove Moyra's mark today, but Selik interrupted me when he paid his little visit. That's why she woke up, but she was never fully awake. If I'd had just a couple more seconds, I could have awakened her completely, and she'd be fine now."

Driskoll looked at Kellach. "Really, Kellach, he's right. I do feel a lot better. This is much better than that weird tea."

Kellach ignored him and glowered at Suma. "If you don't tell me what's going on right now—"

Suma interrupted him. "You'll put a spell on me?" He shook his head. "Sorry, it won't work. I didn't see your punch coming because I can't see objects very well. But I can see magic clearly when it threatens me."

"Like today?" Driskoll asked. "When that snake attacked Kellach, you destroyed it, didn't you?"

Suma looked down. "Yeah. You see I'm learning to be a Yuan-ti cleric. My father is a high priest, so I'm sort of powerful when it comes to magic."

Kellach sputtered something that Driskoll couldn't understand.

But Driskoll had lots of things to say. He wanted to know all about Suma. "Do you—do you have a name?" he stuttered.

"My name in the Yuan-ti language is unpronounceable for you. But Suma is fine. I like it. In fact, I'm thinking of starting a new life somewhere. Maybe I'll just go by Suma."

"Starting a new life?" Driskoll asked, startled. "What do you mean? Where are you going?"

Suma waved it aside. "Forget about it," he said. "We really need to find Moyra. Now."

Driskoll still wasn't sure he comprehended this new turn of events. "So you're really my . . . I mean, you're a snake? You can change from a snake to a person?"

"Uh huh. It's part of our powers."

"Your evil powers?" Kellach growled.

Suma shrugged. "It's true most Yuan-ti have a ruthless nature. But not me. This dream stealing is all Selik's doing. He'll do anything to please Fosh.

"Selik has drawn your whole city to the Westgate. He's opened it up and everyone is going through it toward Fosh's temple beneath the ruins. Soon they will be surrendering their dreams to Fosh. And then, well . . . you can't live without your dreams."

This was too much for Kellach and he started sputtering again. Driskoll heard him say something about getting there on his own.

"But I've got a better plan," Suma said.

Kellach was about to argue with him, but the torch went out and lightning flashed. Driskoll felt himself fall to the earth with a loud bang as if he were a human icicle shattering on impact with the earth. Agonizing pain followed, shooting through his body, starting at his toes and working its way up to his teeth.

He couldn't see anything, but he heard Suma's voice next to him. "You're going to have to trust me."

CHAPTER

20

D riskoll felt his blood run cold—literally.

He felt like he was being stretched out and shrunken at the same time. And just when he felt like he could bear the pain no longer, it was gone. All that remained was a numb coldness inside and out.

Driskoll sensed the ground beneath him. He felt himself stretched out across it. Oh no, he thought desperately. I'm going to sleep, just like everyone else. He tried to raise his head and have a look around, but it was dark, and all he could see were vague, blurry shapes.

Falling had probably dazed him, he thought. He would be able to see clearly again soon. But when he tried to focus his eyes, everything remained in shadow.

Something was moving nearby. For some reason, just the fact that it was moving made it easier to see. It was only a few leaves blowing across the ground in a breeze, but as soon as they settled, he couldn't see them anymore.

Driskoll tried to get up. He knew some part of his body was responding, but he wasn't sure which. Maybe his toes were wiggling. He was so numb he couldn't tell.

But lying on the ground, he was aware of all sorts of strange thumpings and vibrations within the earth itself, which he had never noticed before. Why was he feeling them now?

"Move," someone whispered.

"What?" He was so caught up in the overall weirdness of his situation that it hadn't even occurred to Driskoll that he could move. But he felt a quivering in the ground to his right and he had an idea that he was supposed to follow it.

He was moving now. I have to be dreaming, he thought. It was the kind of dream where you know you're moving, but you can't feel your legs beneath you.

"You're not dreaming," a voice said, as if it had read his thoughts. "Follow me."

Driskoll could barely see anything but he was certain of two things: He knew Kellach and Suma were with him, and he knew that he was still in his own front yard.

"There's a conduit nearby," the voice whispered again. "That will take us to the temple."

Driskoll recognized the voice as Suma's, and at that moment he understood what had happened.

"You turned us into snakes?" Kellach shouted.

From out of nowhere a drum began beating quickly and loudly nearby. Driskoll sensed somehow it was Kellach's body beating the earth in anger.

Driskoll perceived Suma moving toward Kellach, and the beating grew faster. "Listen," Suma hissed. "This is the fastest way to get to Moyra and everyone else."

Of all the strange things going on, the most disconcerting was the fact that although Driskoll couldn't see Kellach and Suma, he could tell them apart from their vibrations as clearly as if he saw them.

Kellach's beating sounds were hard, loud thumps, while Suma made a soft *ticka-ticka-ticka* sound.

Kellach thumped harder. "Turn us back," he hissed.

"But you have to get to Moyra and the others," Suma returned. "They're in the Yuan-ti temple."

"We can get to them on our own," Kellach snarled. "As humans. Now turn us back." His thumping sounds grew louder.

"Come on, Kellach," Driskoll chimed in. "How many people can say they got to be snakes for a day?"

"Driskoll," Kellach spat. "This isn't supposed to be fun. He's turned us into creatures. That means we're under his power."

"Look," Suma interrupted. "I know you don't trust me, Kellach. But your entire city is on its way to Fosh right now. If you follow them you'll have to get past Fosh's guards, and that will put you to sleep or maybe get you killed. Go my way—the snake's way—and you can get there unharmed."

"No," Kellach grumbled. "I don't trust snakes."

"But you are one now," Driskoll pointed out.

Kellach sputtered and swore. "This is all your fault, Driskoll. If you hadn't wanted a stupid pet in the first place—"

"Please, Kellach," Suma pleaded calmly. "This is the only way."

Driskoll felt Suma's vibrations moving away and he followed

them. He could hear Kellach's strong vibrations growing fainter as he felt himself slithering along the ground. He thought for sure he was going to cry, but there weren't any tears, and he guessed that snakes don't weep.

Then a hard, angry thumping sound approached from behind. He recognized it immediately.

"I thought you weren't coming," Driskoll muttered.

"Have to look out for you," Kellach answered in a tight voice.

"Thanks," Driskoll said.

"Come on," Suma called from up ahead. "It's not far."

Driskoll followed in Suma's direction. He knew he was gliding along the ground, although he still couldn't see much besides a sort of gray fog. He slid painlessly over sticks and rocks. In fact, he couldn't feel much except a coldness within him that made him want to find something warm to lie on. Driskoll sensed that they were moving into their backyard.

Suma stopped. "This is where we enter," he said.

Driskoll could feel Suma's vibrations beneath him and he knew that Suma had gone beneath the ground somehow.

He panicked. How would he ever follow Suma now? How would he even find him? Suma's vibrations were moving farther away and deeper into the earth, and with that, his chances of finding Dad and Moyra were slipping away. Driskoll looked around, but he forgot that he couldn't see anything.

Then something deep inside Driskoll told him what to do. It wasn't a voice or anything, more like a feeling. This must be a snake instinct, he thought as he stuck his tongue out and felt the ground with it.

It was amazing. Driskoll immediately knew where he was and what sorts of obstacles were in his way, such as little pebbles or sticks. It felt like the most natural thing in the world to be sticking his tongue out and feeling the ground with it.

When his tongue found a spot where the ground stopped, he knew it was the opening that Suma had passed through seconds earlier. He slipped inside and he felt Kellach behind him. Kellach must have figured it out too.

Driskoll felt himself moving through a narrow tunnel that sloped downward.

"Where are we?" he called ahead to Suma.

"Snake hole," Suma answered. "One of our conduits has been broken, so we've been finding other ways into your city. Fireplaces have been best. A lot of the older ones have tunnels built into them—like at the cathedral and at the blacksmith's. And they're warm too. We like that. But after Kellach fixed the fireplace at Selik's, everyone's gone back to the old way in."

"So you come and go through Selik's fireplace?"

"Right, but Selik's is too far away for us right now, and besides, Fosh's guards are all over it. This is a back route to the Yuan-ti temple."

Kellach grunted in reply. As they slid along in silence, Driskoll was aware of everything—of the mysterious forces of the earth that pulled him toward it, of a million smells coming at him from every direction.

He became aware of subtle differences in the air temperature. They passed through a warm area where they all lingered for a moment. Then a few minutes later, the air grew colder.

"I'm awfully tired all of a sudden," Driskoll said.

"It's the cold air," Suma explained. "Our instincts tell us to sleep when it gets too cold."

"Do you dream when you sleep?" Driskoll asked.

Suma stopped. "No, snakes can't dream. And dreams are what make you humans creative. They're inspiration. They can help you sort out your problems. That's why Fosh wants to steal them. He thinks it will make him even greater than he already is. But the fact is, humans need dreams to survive. You'll die without them."

"And I'm guessing your friend Fosh doesn't care about that?" Kellach growled.

"Nope, not a bit. That's why he came up with the clay pots."

"Which you destroyed," Driskoll said.

"Of course," Suma answered. "I was supposed to collect your dreams in those pots Selik gave you. But I wouldn't do it." He chuckled. "In fact, from what I've heard, all the Yuan-ti are pretty impressed that you two have avoided the dream stealing. You're quite a catch right now."

"What do you mean?" Kellach asked suspiciously.

"I mean there are a lot of Yuan-ti who'd like to show Fosh that they managed to steal the dreams of the last two holdouts in town. Fosh wants the dreams of every single citizen of Curston. And he's very angry that you have the mark, but he doesn't have your dreams yet."

"So what does the mark mean?"

"The mark of the Yuan-ti?" Suma sounded uncomfortable. "When a Yuan-ti snake bites you, you're under our control. That mark is our way of showing that we own your dreams. When the Yuan-ti cleric comes, he knows he can take dreams from someone with that mark."

"'We'?" Kellach interjected. "'We'? So you admit you do this."

Suma shook his head. "I've never bitten a human, and I would never do it unless it was it in self-defense."

"Hmpf," Kellach grunted.

They slid into an open room with many different smells—human smells. Driskoll was able to single out one scent in particular.

"Moyra!" Driskoll whispered. "It's like I can sense her. How am I doing that?"

"Your sense of smell is your most powerful tool," Suma explained. "But you're not smelling with any kind of a nose like humans have. It's your tongue. A snake's tongue can take in thousands of smells. And because it is shaped like a Y, it picks up scents from all directions. It allows us to zero in on our prey."

"You know, I hate to interrupt this little chat," Kellach cut in, "but might I remind you, Driskoll, that you are under this snake's power right now? Let's try to keep the conversations to a minimum."

"That's fine," Suma said. "We're almost at the main temple."

"And then you'll turn us back into our human selves?" Kellach asked.

"I think we should surprise Fosh and his guards," Suma said. "So let's wait until we get inside. What do you think, Driskoll?"

"Sounds good to me," Driskoll agreed.

Kellach sighed loudly. Driskoll guessed that Suma had slid around and was facing him. He could make out a green blur that must have been Suma.

"Now when we get inside the temple, if you don't want to get killed by the guards, just follow my lead. Then when the Inevitable comes—"

"Did you just say the Inevitable?" Driskoll gulped.

"He brought the Inevitable here. He's betrayed us," Kellach hissed. "I knew it."

"I haven't betrayed you," Suma said. "You control the Inevitable."

"That's ridiculous," Kellach spat. "It's looking for the Knights of the Silver Dragon. That's us."

Suma snickered. "Yeah, it's looking for you all right."

"And you've brought it here to find us?" Kellach shrieked.

"Well, I didn't exactly bring it here," Suma said. "After Driskoll destroyed it over at Selik's, I went back in and told it my plan. It can actually understand, you know. Anyway, it should be here as soon as it rebuilds itself."

"You creepy little snake!" Kellach shouted. "What did I tell you, Driskoll? You can't trust snakes."

Driskoll was beside himself. "I don't get it, Suma," he said. "Why would you betray us to the Inevitable? I though you were my friend."

"What?" Suma sounded surprised. "I am your friend. And I didn't betray you. I'm helping you."

Kellach's thumpings were so loud Driskoll could barely hear Suma.

"We should get moving," Suma said. "We can talk as we go."

But Kellach wasn't moving. "Do you actually think we're going anywhere else with you?" Kellach was almost laughing he was so angry. "Turn us back into humans."

"But what about my plan? We can get inside there and then the Inevitable—"

"You won't get away with your plan, you dirty snake," Kellach said. "Now, I demand you turn us back."

Driskoll was so confused he thought he might be sick. He didn't know what to think. This was Suma. His pet. His friend. He had trusted him. Could he still trust Suma?

"It might help us trust you a little more if you just turned us back into humans," Driskoll said finally.

Suma hesitated. "Okay," he said slowly. "But you will have to be really, really quiet. Fosh's guards will be able to feel your vibrations and they'll know you're human."

"Just do it," Kellach hissed.

Suddenly Driskoll felt an excruciating pain, as if a lightning bolt jolted his bones. But instead of a cold shock, now it felt like hot lava pouring through him.

Then just as before, the pain stopped. Driskoll looked around. He could see clearly again. He was still on the floor, but he was aware of arms and legs—his own. He was also very warm.

And he could see clearly now. They were in a small, window-less chamber that was dimly lit by torches that revealed more paintings on the walls. Driskoll caught a glimpse of a rather gruesome scene showing a snake eating something.

He turned away and saw Kellach—a human Kellach—lying next to him on the gravel floor, grimacing. Then Kellach's pained face relaxed a little and Driskoll wobbled to his feet. Suma—the boy Suma—stood in front of him, supporting him. Suma turned to Kellach and helped him up too. Then he put his hands on his hips and grinned at them.

"Well? What did you think of being a snake for a while?"

"Here's what I think," Kellach said. He pulled his fist back to punch Suma, but Suma was ready this time.

He grabbed Kellach around the neck and with one arm, lifted him off the floor. Then he put him down.

"Sorry," he said. "But we shouldn't cause any commotion. Fosh's guards are everywhere along this route and—"

Kellach swore loudly and started in for Suma again.

"Be quiet!" Suma whispered, desperately reaching again for Kellach.

"Too late," a deep voice said behind him. Driskoll turned. A figure stood in a shadowy doorway. The figure took a step into the room and Driskoll recognized the tan, tattooed face immediately.

Selik. He stared at all of them, his eyes shining like he'd discovered a very valuable piece of artwork. Two huge black snakes flanked him on either side. Selik smiled.

"Come in," he said. "Fosh is waiting for you."

CHAPTER

21

"Don't move," Suma whispered to Driskoll and Kellach. "Just follow my lead, and I'll protect you."

The two black snakes slithered forward and stopped at the boys' feet. The reptiles coiled themselves into striking poses and hissed.

Two more snakes entered and crept toward Suma. He gave them a threatening look and they backed away. Selik rubbed his chin and gazed coldly at Suma, who stared back at him.

Selik turned his attention to the snakes and uttered a strange syllable. It sounded like he gave them an order. Selik glanced at Suma and spoke again, nodding at Kellach and Driskoll. It was definitely a different language and it sounded like another order.

"He says we're supposed to go into the next chamber," Suma said in a flat voice.

Selik uttered something else that Driskoll didn't understand.

"Oh," Suma added, looking down at his feet. "He says that if you try to escape, the snakes will kill you."

Selik nodded his head, indicating that they were all to go through the door behind him. Driskoll noticed that while two large snakes were shadowing him and Kellach, Suma did not have a snake following at his heels.

Suma looked hard at Driskoll as he passed him, as if he were trying to tell Driskoll something.

They walked slowly through a doorway and into yet another sloping tunnel. They hadn't walked fifty paces when they passed through another door. They entered a room full of statues.

With a closer look, Driskoll realized that these weren't statues. These were people—live people, or maybe sleeping people. They were all citizens of Curston, and not one of them moved or made a sound. They each wore that glassy, zombie-like stare, and their skin was slightly gray, as if they were made of stone. They simply stood there, each one holding a clay pot.

There were watchers in full uniform next to merchants in aprons. Faithful clerics stood next to hardened prisoners in chains. Half-orcs, elves and humans; children, parents and grand-parents—they were all stuffed as tight as fish in a basket.

For a moment, Driskoll thought he saw Torin's dark head high above the rest, but he couldn't be sure. He shivered. Walking by hundreds of rows of silently staring people was eerie. Driskoll felt he was disturbing them somehow, although they did not seem to notice him at all.

He noticed that Suma did not stare, but walked along with his head bowed. Selik on the other hand, looked at the rows with a cold, calculating eye. He spotted Driskoll looking at him and smiled. "There are two other chambers identical to this one that are full of them. They are here to deliver their dreams to Fosh."

A horrible thought struck Driskoll. This was a storage room of some kind—for people. They kept walking past the rows until they came to yet another door. Selik spoke as they walked.

"We have waited a long time for this day," he said. "I've had to endure your kind for years while we perfected our skills."

"You were the spy for Fosh," Suma said.

"A proud job for a proud cause," Selik answered airily. "And as you know, my job is my life—except when I had to interact with the humans. Fosh knows it was beneath me. He favored me with gifts to repay me," he said with a hard look at Suma.

"You seemed to think we humans were okay when you could steal stuff from us," Kellach said.

"Well, yes, of course. But what is the point?" Selik answered. "Humans are only worth something when they can give us something."

"Like dreams," Driskoll added.

"Oh, and by the way," Selik said. "I know your friend stole my journal, the little thief."

"I thought you people approved of stealing," Driskoll shot back.

"Oh, I do approve, I do," Selik answered. "That's why I've given your friend Moyra a special pass to go to the front of the line. She's probably surrendering her dreams to Fosh right now."

Suma finally glanced up. He looked like he was about to say something, but they had stopped in front of a door, which Selik unlocked. They all passed through it and entered yet another chamber.

But this was completely different. It was a huge, open room. Row after row of stone columns stretched to a towering ceiling at least five-hundred feet in the air.

The absence of windows reinforced the fact that they were still underground. Gigantic wall torches and a bonfire in the center of the chamber gave the place an eerie orange glow. The air itself was thick with a sickeningly sweet incense, and although it was hard to see details clearly through the haze, Driskoll couldn't miss the room's dominant feature: a huge, black stone statue of a giant serpent getting ready to strike a considerably smaller and obviously terrified man. It was easy to see who the Yuan-ti thought were in charge of things.

This must be the temple Suma was talking about, Driskoll thought.

Suma quickened his pace as soon as he entered. He held his head high and he almost looked like he was swaggering the way Kellach often did.

Kellach and Driskoll had both stopped. Suma glanced back and motioned for them to follow him and Selik down a long aisle in the center of the floor. The snakes behind them hissed, and Driskoll jumped forward. Suma looked back and grinned at Driskoll.

A sea of snakes surrounded them on both sides. Some were coiled around the columns, but most were crawling, slithering and writhing along the floor. A few human-like creatures that resembled Suma stood here and there among them, watching the boys with hypnotic-looking yellow eyes.

Suma had said that all of the Yuan-ti were gathered here, and Driskoll believed it. There were thousands more than he had seen in St. Cuthbert's earlier.

Suma and Selik walked past the snakes, which slithered out of the way to form a clear path. Driskoll and Kellach followed as they headed for the front of the chamber, where there was an altar or a kind of stage. It was raised about six feet off the ground, with no visible steps leading up to it.

The altar ran the length of the front of the room, and the top of it was alive with movement. A few human-looking servants scuttled around it, and some large snakes slithered back and forth along the edge like guards on patrol.

A large black lump sat on a sort of throne in the center of the altar. There were two yellow, unblinking eyes in the center of it. It was the biggest snake Driskoll had ever seen. Its head alone was the size of a large boulder, and Driskoll guessed its body was more than fifteen feet long. This had to be Fosh.

A small line of about twenty people stretched in front of the altar and down on the ground, where the rest of them stood. They looked like they were from the storage room the boys had just passed through, and they stared straight ahead like zombies. Each one in turn placed a clay pot on a black table at the foot of the altar.

As each person left his or her pot on it, the table rose up, and Driskoll realized that it wasn't a table. It was a long, thick snake. It balanced each pot on its head as it uncoiled itself and rose higher and higher until it was level with the altar. Then it left the pot on the edge where a human-looking servant appeared from out of nowhere and took it. The servant brought the pot to the big snake and laid it on the altar before him. Driskoll couldn't tell for sure, but it looked like hundreds of pots were already lined up in rows on the altar.

He looked at the line of people presenting the clay pots. Toward the front of the line, a flash of red hair caught Driskoll's eye. Moyra. She stood with everyone else, clutching a clay pot and staring blindly ahead. She obviously had no idea where she was or what she was doing.

Suma and Selik swept past the line of people and knelt at the foot of the altar before the snake. Neither of them spoke. Selik bowed his head while Suma looked boldly at the big snake. It turned its massive head in Suma's direction and stared back at him.

It stared for a long, long time, and Driskoll could see that Suma didn't move. Then the snake began speaking. Driskoll knew what Suma had meant when he'd said that his name was unpronounceable. He couldn't even see how a human mouth could form the hisses and guttural sounds the great snake was making. But he didn't need to speak Yuan-ti to know that the old snake was telling Suma off.

When the snake finally finished ranting, Suma turned and looked at Driskoll. There was a funny look in his eye. Then Suma turned back to the great snake and addressed him in a language Driskoll understood.

"Look, Father," he said. "I have made up for my foolish behavior. I bring you the last two humans from the town."

Driskoll was confused. He was pretty sure Suma had just called Fosh his father.

"And now, Father," Suma went on, "I offer them to you. I

offer you their dreams—the last dreams of the city. The dreams of the Knights of the Silver Dragon."

There was a hush in the room, and the great snake laughed in a very nasty way. "Is that true? These puny little creatures are all that are left of the Knights?"

The snake laughed again. "If we'd known that this was all Zendric had to defend that rotten little city, I would have taken their dreams long ago."

"It is a great mistake to underestimate them, Father." Suma said. "These two have eluded your dream stealers. But I knew what would draw them to you."

"Very good." The great snake nodded its head and looked at Driskoll and Kellach. He turned back to Suma. "This is a sign to me that you have indeed made up for your serious errors. You may set my guards on them."

Driskoll could feel Kellach tense up next to him. He didn't need to look around to know that several huge snakes had begun moving toward them.

He stared at Suma, who shot a sly grin back.

"Never trust a snake," Suma said.

CHAPTER

22

K ellach glared at Driskoll, and this time, Driskoll knew he
deserved it. This is all my fault, he thought miserably.

The snakes moved closer, but Driskoll kept his eyes on Suma,
who was now glancing around the chamber.

"Yes," Selik said. "My young brother has done fine work—
for once."

"Your brother?" Driskoll said aloud.

"Of course," Selik answered. "Fosh has thousands of children. But our youngest brother has always been worthless. He
refused to participate in the dream stealing, which is why we
set the wolves on him. But now he has redeemed himself in the
eyes of the Yuan-ti."

Selik turned back to Suma. "Now it is complete," he said.
"With your help, we will soon have seized all of the dreams."

Suma spoke up as his eyes still searched the room. "Without
their dreams, they will all die," he said.

"But that is a small cost to us," Selik finished, staring hard at him. "They will suit our father and give him all that he needs."

There was movement on the platform behind Selik. A human-looking servant was removing the lid from one of the pots on the altar. He held it up to Fosh. The great snake opened its mouth, revealing long, sharp fangs. The servant poured the colorful substance inside the snake's huge, gaping mouth.

Fosh was taking someone's dream. It was horrible to watch all of those beautiful stars and colorful images swallowed up by that hulking monster, and Driskoll had to turn away.

He looked again at Suma, but the boy was still looking around the temple. He could have sworn Suma looked nervous. But Driskoll didn't care. Suma had betrayed him. He felt two snakes coil themselves around his ankles.

Selik was coming closer, surrounded by more snakes. "You are the last to surrender your dreams. But don't worry, it will be painless."

Driskoll looked at him in disbelief.

"Ah," Selik smiled. "You are finally learning to question me. You are right this time. I lied. It will actually be very painful."

He shot a look at the snake behind Kellach. There was a hiss and Kellach gasped. Then Kellach fell to the floor and didn't move.

"Kellach!" Driskoll shouted. He strained against the snakes coiled tightly around him, but they wouldn't budge.

"Oh, he's not dead, if that's what you're thinking," Selik said casually. "He has been bitten. You small Knights seem to require a stronger venom, one that will put you to sleep instantly."

Selik looked at Kellach, asleep on the floor and surrounded by two snakes. "Soon we will collect his dreams," he said, glancing up at Driskoll. "That will be a sight for you to see."

Driskoll stared, horrified. He could not believe what was happening.

These people are crazy, Driskoll thought. And they were about the most evil creatures he had ever encountered. But he didn't see any way out. The snakes were wrapped around him tight as heavy ropes. And even if he could break free, there were thousands of snakes in here ready to kill him the moment he looked cross-eyed at them.

Then there was the matter of Kellach, Moyra, and the rest of Curston waiting just outside. Even if he were to somehow break free, and even if the snakes miraculously didn't bother him, how would he awaken the others and get them out of here?

His heart pumping wildly, Driskoll looked around. They were surrounded by snakes of every size—all glaring at him with hungry eyes. Up on the altar, Fosh ignored him as he swallowed another dream.

Selik watched Driskoll, an odd smile playing at the corner of his lips. "You are the only one who does not bear the mark of the Yuan-ti," he said. "But that is of no consequence. You shall receive it now."

Driskoll knew what was coming next. There was nothing he could do—he couldn't even move. All of his dreams, and all the dreams of everyone in Curston, were about to be swallowed up. But first, the bite would come.

Selik clapped his hands and the snake behind him hissed. Driskoll felt a knife in his leg as a snake jabbed its teeth into him for the second time that day. He doubled over. He could feel the venom shooting up his body.

He was furious with himself for coming under the Yuan-ti's control. He tensed himself against the sleepiness that would soon wash over him. But strangely, he wasn't tired. He looked around. The snakes were all looking at him in anticipation.

Sure, he felt a little sleepy, but he didn't feel those overpowering waves of weariness and fatigue that seemed to carry him away earlier. He just felt a little out of sorts, and that was all. It was very confusing. He looked down at the snake that had bit him. Maybe it hadn't given him the right venom. And then he noticed his hands. They were still shaking. Kellach's potion, he thought. I bet that's why I'm not feeling tired. Kellach said it would last a while. He smirked to himself. That's one kind of magic these Yuan-ti can't beat.

"What's wrong?" Fosh demanded from up on the altar. "Why isn't he asleep?"

Selik studied Driskoll. "I-I don't know."

"What did you do this time?" The big snake snarled. He launched into a tirade against Selik in that strange language. Again, Driskoll couldn't understand it, but he knew from the way Selik hung his head and winced that Fosh was saying all sorts of horrible, humiliating things to him.

Driskoll thought of his own father. Sure, Torin yelled at Driskoll a lot, but never in such a mean-spirited way as Fosh was doing now. Fosh made Torin look like a gentle puppy.

When Fosh finally finished, Selik clapped his hands again at the snake curled around Driskoll. Another knife-like fang pierced Driskoll's leg, and the pain shot through him like lightning. This bite was even more painful than the first, and he began to feel weak.

"Here it comes," he thought. This time, the venom seemed to have worked.

Still, Driskoll didn't feel nearly as tired. Maybe he wasn't going to be controlled so easily.

Slowly, though, a change moved through him. He felt alone, desperately alone. The temple and the snakes were gone. Kellach and Moyra were gone. Driskoll was the only living creature left in the world.

If this was a dream, it was the strangest one he'd ever had. There was nothing here. No silvery stars, no colorful images. Everything was completely black. But somewhere at the bottom of the deep abyss into which he was falling, he felt something—a tickle, maybe, or a vibration on his toes.

He couldn't see anything really, but he sensed a presence. He wasn't alone after all. Suma was there.

Suma, the traitor. Suma, the person he had trusted, but who had brought him here to surrender his dreams to the horrible black snake.

Suma was grinning with his usual wide, toothy smile.

"What do you want?" Driskoll felt himself ask. But he didn't speak it. After all, he was dreaming.

Suma shook his head. "Nothing," he said. "I don't want anything. And neither should you. Just keep thinking of nothing."

"What?"

"I don't know what that potion of Kellach's did to you, but you're not dreaming, and that's good. Just keep telling yourself that there's nothing here. They can't take your dreams if you don't have any."

Driskoll didn't know what Suma was talking about, but he

was beginning to like the feeling of nothingness. At least it was helping him forget the snakes. He wanted to look away from Suma, but Suma's voice was inside his head.

"Just hold on a little longer," Suma said. "It'll be here any minute."

Then Suma was gone. Driskoll couldn't feel the vibrations anymore, but he couldn't think either. What had Suma just said? He couldn't remember anything. It felt like there was nothing in his head but an empty black space.

Driskoll tried to concentrate, but the empty feeling spread over his entire body like a black blanket.

Dimly, he began to sense a noise, a heavy, clanking noise like a huge metal chain. The blackness began to lighten. Soon it was more like a thick fog, and a pair of mechanical golden eyes flashed in front of him.

Driskoll suddenly had the distinct impression that this wasn't a dream. The snakes were back—he was in the temple. The Inevitable had broken through a wall and was crashing over the snakes. Its eyes were fixed on Driskoll, and its chained arms rose over its head. It held something aloft.

Driskoll's sword.

Driskoll felt fully awake now as he saw the gleaming blade carried toward him in the hand of the Inevitable. How had he awakened? He caught a glimpse of Suma, staring intensely at him, his hands raised in the air. But all around Suma there was confusion as hundreds of snakes backed away from the crashing, trampling Inevitable.

The next second, Suma was lost in the commotion. The snakes that were coiled around Driskoll's legs tightened their grip in terror. Driskoll started to feel lightheaded just as Kellach stirred next to him.

"Kellach!" Driskoll cried. "The Inevitable!"

But Kellach was still sleeping. Driskoll didn't know what to do now. The Inevitable had his sword, and Driskoll was without the iron poker. He was too far away from the bonfire to try and confuse it with smoke. The Inevitable clanked closer every second and Driskoll was out of ideas. He couldn't even reason with the creature.

Or could he?

He remembered what Suma had said. He controlled the Inevitable. But could Driskoll believe Suma? He looked around, but he couldn't see Suma anywhere. The Inevitable was only a few paces from him. If Suma had been lying to him, then there was nothing Driskoll could do about it now.

His heart was thundering inside of him, and he couldn't think of anything else to say. "Don't attack me," Driskoll yelled. "Get them!" He pointed at the snakes. "They're the ones who are evil."

Selik screamed as Driskoll continued pointing at the snakes. They all slithered away, tumbling over each other in a desperate desire to escape.

The Inevitable stopped. It focused its inhuman eyes on Driskoll and took a step closer. Well, that's it, Driskoll thought, still pointing at the snakes. I didn't think it would work anyway.

The Inevitable's gears moved as it focused not on Driskoll's face, but on his pin. The Knights of the Silver Dragon pin. Driskoll looked down at it. The Inevitable brought its massive arm slowly down in front of Driskoll. The sword glinted in the palm of its golden hand. It would be easy for Driskoll to reach out and grab it.

This was very confusing. It was almost as if the Inevitable was giving him his sword. He looked at the golden eyes. They stared lifelessly, but intelligently, at him.

Driskoll reached out and with a shaking hand grasped his sword. The Inevitable didn't move.

But as soon as Driskoll had his sword, the hulking golden creature was in action again. It reared around and picked up a nearby snake and hurled it across the chamber.

"I knew he'd come!" a voice yelled. It was Suma. He was standing at Driskoll's shoulder, beaming at Driskoll excitedly. "I knew he'd find you. Now you can command him to destroy them all."

Driskoll was really confused now. He had thought Suma was his friend, but Suma had betrayed him. And now, Suma seemed to be on Driskoll's side again.

The Inevitable picked up another snake and hurled it toward the altar. Suma cheered. Most of the snakes cowered away, but some of the bigger ones were coiling around its legs, trying to bite it. But it did no good. What snakes the Inevitable didn't step on, it threw at the altar or into the bonfire. It was destroying them all.

The snakes around Driskoll's feet had fallen away and he could move again. He ducked through the mayhem and managed to find Kellach. He dragged him over to the platform near where Moyra and the others stood. None of them seemed aware of the violence happening all around them.

"Come on, there's shelter up there," someone shouted in his ear. He turned and saw Suma staring at Moyra. He was levitating her up onto the altar. But instead of using his arms like Kellach did, he simply stared at her. He guided her to a spot in a corner and laid her down gently on the floor of the altar.

Driskoll gently pushed some of the townspeople to the front of the altar, where Suma stared at each one of them, levitating them up. Fosh had mysteriously disappeared from the altar, but Selik was up there running around, looking for someplace to hide.

"Do something," Selik shouted at Suma.

"Okay," Suma said as he moved the last of the sleepers—Kellach—up onto the altar. He grabbed Driskoll's arm and Driskoll felt himself lifted up onto the altar.

Suma looked at the rows and rows of clay pots in front of Fosh's empty throne.

"Come on," he yelled back to Driskoll. "We've got to destroy these." He stomped down hard, shattering a pot and sending out a brilliant fountain of purple stars. Selik screamed and ran away as Suma jumped on another pot.

"Don't you see?" he yelled at Driskoll. "Fosh can't get these dreams if we release them."

Driskoll watched for a moment as Suma jumped up and down, destroying the pots. Silver stars flew everywhere, dissolving in the air.

"You can always trust a snake to have plans beneath plans beneath plans," Suma yelled breathlessly. "I knew you could order the Inevitable to destroy the Yuan-ti and stop their dream thieving."

It was hard to hear over the crashing, screaming, and general mayhem, but Driskoll wanted to understand a few things. "How did you know the Inevitable would come here?"

"The Inevitable only says the name of its master," Suma explained. "It doesn't reveal its prey. That's what makes it so terrifying. You find out in your last living moment who sent the Inevitable to kill you."

"So the reason the Inevitable kept saying 'Knights of the Silver Dragon' was that it wanted us to command it? We are its masters?"

"Exactly. Remember your friend Zendric's note? It said 'Inevitable—show Silver Dragon . . . ' The Inevitable saw your Silver Dragon pin at the blacksmith's shop. And it stopped when it got close to you. Later, I heard you talking in your room about the Inevitable. When I heard Kellach tell you that it was saying 'Knights of the Silver Dragon' over and over, I knew you were its masters. That's when I got the idea to bring you here and have the Inevitable destroy the Yuan-ti."

"So you didn't bring us here to offer us up to your father."

"No way," Suma answered. "I had to think fast when my brother and the other guards found us."

"Why didn't you tell us Fosh was your father?"

Suma stopped and looked at Driskoll. "I guess I was embarrassed," he said. Driskoll certainly understood that. If Fosh were his father, he would have left town long ago.

Driskoll stood at the rear of the altar near Moyra, Kellach, and the townspeople. They were beginning to stir, and he moved away from them so that the crashing pots wouldn't injure them.

He could see beyond Suma down into the temple where the Inevitable was trampling and throwing the snakes around. Driskoll went back to work crushing the pots, when out of nowhere, he heard the clanking growing closer. He looked up. The Inevitable was at the altar, just in front of Suma, and almost level with him.

Suma's back was toward the Inevitable. He was so engrossed in stomping that he didn't notice the monstrous creature behind him. It reached out its armored hands toward Suma, and Driskoll understood.

The Inevitable could see that Suma was a Yuan-ti. The chained arm headed straight down, directly at Suma's head.

CHAPTER

23

Driskoll jumped in front of the creature.

"No!" he shouted raising an arm to stop it. "Don't touch him."

The Inevitable stopped and focused its metallic golden eyes up toward Driskoll. Then they swiveled toward Suma and back to Driskoll. Its arms began moving up and down, and the chain came out and then retracted.

Suma whipped around and saw what was happening. "It's confused," he murmured. "First you told it to destroy us, but now you've told it not to. It can't handle conflicting information."

Pieces of alabaster armor began to shoot out from the Inevitable, hitting a few of the snakes. The mighty creature tilted from one side to the other, and its eyes spun in their sockets. Wires snapped and smoke puffed. Then with a loud tearing creak, the Inevitable's legs buckled, and it crashed to the ground.

Everything in the room stopped. Several escaping snakes seemed to catch wind of what was happening and began to head back toward the altar. Driskoll could see it in their eyes. They knew their enemy had been defeated, and they knew who had set the Inevitable on them in the first place.

Before Driskoll could move, hundreds of snakes were on the altar, closing in on Driskoll and Suma.

A deep voice behind them spoke, and Driskoll didn't have to turn around to know who it was.

Fosh had reappeared.

Fosh surveyed the broken pots all over the platform and hissed loudly, but it was more like the roar of an angry lion. His eyes shone with a ghostly yellow light, and he fixed a terrifying stare on Suma. He sped toward him.

Suma grabbed Driskoll's arm and moved them both determinedly over to where Kellach, Moyra, and the townspeople were. Kellach had awakened a little and looked up groggily.

Then Suma picked up a broken pot and held it up to the giant snake.

"This is where it ends," he said.

A huge black hood whipped out from Fosh's neck. He hissed threateningly at Suma. "You are no longer Yuan-ti. You are no longer my son," the big snake snarled. "You will die with your human friends."

The rest of the snakes had formed a kind of moving, reptilian wall all around the kids. The snakes moved, one on top of the other, slithering in and out, but never breaking the circle. Hundreds of pairs of eyes stared hungrily at Driskoll.

Fosh sat inside the circle a few feet from the kids. Suma looked defiantly at him and held his arms out wide. "I'm not afraid to die," Suma said in a strong but shaky voice. "But you must stop this dream stealing. You can kill me, but don't hurt my friends."

Fosh laughed a sinister sort of bellowing noise. "You are in no position to tell me who lives and who dies."

Moyra was starting to awaken. She stretched but didn't open her eyes. "Where in the name of gargoyles are we?" she asked loudly. "And what's going on?" She opened her eyes and saw the snakes circling her. It took a second before she realized what was happening and she jumped up between Driskoll and Suma.

Fosh advanced toward them, his mouth open wide in a murderous fury, and the circle of snakes grew tighter around the kids.

"No time to explain," Driskoll whispered to her as the snakes moved closer.

Kellach had awakened and was trying to stand up. The three of them and Suma formed a tight little group near the broken pots as the snakes circled.

"Seems like every time I try to get a little sleep, some creepy snake comes after me," Moyra whispered.

"Sleep." Driskoll stared at her. "Sleep. That's what they need."

He turned to Kellach. "Get it? They need to sleep."

Fosh and the snakes stopped moving for a moment as if to savor their victims' terror.

"Kellach," Driskoll whispered again. He didn't care that the snakes could hear him. This was their only chance, and Kellach didn't seem to be getting it. "Remember how tired you were when we went through that cold spot a little while ago? What if it got really, really cold in here?"

Kellach stared blankly for a moment, and Driskoll was sure his brother didn't understand. He glanced around. A particularly large silver snake had broken away from the wall and slithered up to Driskoll.

Kellach shook his head. "I know what you're trying to do," he said. "But they can sense magic. Suma said so."

Driskoll could feel the tongue of the silver snake darting in and out, jabbing at his legs. The snake was playing with him, teasing him. Any second now, it would strike.

The snakes didn't seem to mind that Driskoll and Kellach were talking. They seemed to sense that no matter what the boys said to each other, they were going to be dead in a few minutes anyway.

"They can beat me at magic," Kellach whispered. "They can see it coming."

Driskoll clenched his fists. Every day of his life, Kellach was showing off his magical abilities. This was no time for him to get shy about it.

"No," he whispered furiously. "They only sense magic when it threatens them. All you're doing is making some ice."

"All right," Kellach said as several snakes skimmed over to him and opened their mouths to strike. "We don't have much else." Kellach waved his arm sleepily. The silver snake wrapped itself around Driskoll, and he cried out in surprise and pain as it squeezed at his legs. The snake looked up at him, and Driskoll was sure it smiled. The creature was enjoying Driskoll's pain.

There was a brilliant flash of white light, and Driskoll wondered if Kellach had gotten it right.

But he looked down, and the stone floor at his feet was gone.

In its place was a shining white sheet of pure, perfect ice. The silver snake slipped drowsily away from his legs. With a faint crackling sound, the ice spread down the sides of the altar, across the massive floor, and up the columns and walls.

It moved like a white tidal wave across the room. It put out the bonfire and covered the giant snake statue. It buried many of the snakes that lay on the floor.

One by one, the snakes surrounding Driskoll and the others slowed down. Driskoll shivered as Selik suddenly looked puzzled. He watched Selik raise his arm and then fall wordlessly to the floor.

Last to go was Fosh. His huge body grew limp. He glared at the kids one last time and then fell forward on the ice.

Moyra cheered. Kellach smiled and folded his arms. "Serves them right," he said. "A taste of their own venom."

Driskoll looked around. Suma was gone.

He had been right next to him on the platform.

"Oh no," Driskoll moaned. "Kellach, can you help me find Suma?"

Kellach stretched. "Wow," he said. "I feel great."

"Kellach," Driskoll said. "I can't find Suma. I think he's underneath all of these snakes."

"Don't worry about it," Kellach said. He pointed at the ice behind Driskoll. Driskoll turned. There on the ice, entwined among several snakes, was a thin green line.

Driskoll peeled the tiny snake away from the others and looked at Kellach.

"He didn't betray us," Driskoll said. "He brought us here so we could make the Inevitable destroy them."

"I know, Kellach answered. "I heard a lot of what was going on."

"You did?"

"Yeah, I had some of that tree bark tea potion too, you know. I think it kept us awake enough to be aware of things."

Driskoll looked down at the handsome green snake in his hands. "He's not dead, is he?"

"Of course not," Kellach smiled. "Just asleep like the rest of them."

"How long will the snakes sleep here?" Moyra asked.

Kellach laughed. "That's a permanent ice spell. It will only wear off if I undo it. We can keep them asleep in here for a long, long time."

Moyra shivered. "That's a good idea," she said. "I don't know how I got here, and I don't like this place."

Driskoll looked at the Inevitable, which was in pieces again on the floor. "It gave me my sword back," Driskoll murmured.

"Yeah, I guess it isn't so bad, as long as it's on our side," Kellach said.

"Think it'll put itself together again soon?" Driskoll asked.

"Yeah," Kellach answered. "But I'm not ready just yet. Are you two?"

Driskoll and Moyra shook their heads. Kellach reached down and picked up a few gears and axles from the pile.

"He can't get very far without these," Kellach said. "We'll give them back to him when we're ready. Now, come on. Let's get out of here."

24

The three kids picked their way over the sleeping snakes and tried to keep from slipping on the ice as they climbed through the hole in the wall made by the Inevitable.

Driskoll carried Suma carefully as they followed the path back up the long corridor, which was also made wider by the Inevitable.

Kellach and Moyra led the confused but wide-awake townspeople out of the temple and into the chamber they had passed through earlier. There were no snakes in here, and no ice either. But hundreds more bewildered townspeople murmured among themselves. Driskoll was relieved that no one had panicked—yet.

He picked up snatches of conversations.

"I'm telling you, Guinevere, I just woke up and here I was. I don't know where that elf maiden came from . . ."

"Well I heard from the Bryce the candle maker that Curston was overrun by grimlocks, and they erased our memory and drove us out . . ."

"It's just like I'm always telling you, Mordred. You can never find the watchers when you need them. Oh, there's a watcher . . . "

Despite the strange surroundings and general confusion, Driskoll was glad to hear other people's voices again.

He felt something wriggle in his hands. He looked down.

Suma was looking up at him. Driskoll smiled, and he was sure that Suma smiled back. He laid the snake on the ground, away from the gathering crowd.

No one else noticed the puff of smoke as Suma appeared, a boy again, grinning at Driskoll.

"That was excellent," Driskoll exclaimed. "Especially when you crushed all of those clay pots and stood up to Fosh."

"Thanks," Suma said. He looked away.

"Uh, I'm sorry." Driskoll felt awkward suddenly. "I know you've lost your family and everything."

"It's okay," Suma said, still looking away.

Driskoll tried to cheer him up a little. "You could stay in Curston," he said. "We've got plenty of room at our house."

Suma turned back to Driskoll and smiled a little. "Thanks," he said. "But I don't like sleeping in a basket."

They both chuckled. "But seriously," Suma said. "There are a few others like me. We've been trying to fight my father for years, and we'd like to start a new life somewhere. But I don't know if people here would trust us."

"Well," Driskoll said. "Once you get rid of these scars for us, it might help."

Suma grinned. "That could take a long time."

Driskoll grinned back. "Right," he said. "Then maybe we'll

have time to get to be better friends."

The boys shook hands as Kellach and Moyra came up. "Have you seen Dad anywhere?" Kellach asked.

"Or my parents?" Moyra added.

Driskoll shook his head. "I haven't seen anybody that I know. And I was wondering about Grayson and his dad. How are they going to rebuild their shop? And how are we going to explain that the Inevitable destroyed it?"

"Hmm," Kellach held up the golden parts of the once mighty Inevitable. "Maybe we should pay a visit here tomorrow. Since we control the Inevitable, maybe we can order it to rebuild the blacksmith's shop."

Ever since Moyra and Kellach had walked up to them, Suma had bowed his head. Now he looked up at Moyra. "I-I can help you find your parents," he said, his face turning slightly pink.

"Okay," Moyra answered. "But first I could use a nap."

The boys stared at her.

"Kidding," she laughed.

Zendric made his way through the crowd and looked at the kids. He regarded Suma coldly for a moment.

"Yuan-ti," he murmured.

"It's okay, Zendric," Kellach reassured him. "He's not a Yuan-ti anymore. He's a friend. He's the one who helped us figure out your message."

"My message?" Zendric asked.

"You were writing to us just before you fell asleep," Kellach explained. "You wrote that we were supposed to show the Inevitable our Knights of the Silver Dragon pin, but you couldn't finish because you fell asleep. Suma here showed us that we could control the Inevitable and make it destroy the Yuan-ti."

"Of course," Zendric said, tapping his head. "My message. Now I remember."

"So how did you know about the Inevitable and the Yuan-ti, Zendric?" Kellach asked.

"Your father called me to the blacksmith's shop with him," the elf explained. "When I saw those snakes coming through the fireplace, I knew they had to be Yuan-ti. I was worried, knowing that there is very little magic that can stop this powerful race. So I summoned the Inevitable to aid us. But then I was bitten and fell under the Yuan-ti's spell. I thought you might have a chance to stop the Yuan-ti, if only you could find the Inevitable. So I went home and wrote my note to you. I knew that I could not make it to your house, but that you would come looking for me."

He nodded at the golden pieces in Kellach's hands. "It looks as if you found me—and the Inevitable," he said.

"Yeah," Kellach answered. He was about to say more, but Torin swept up to them. "What are you three doing here?" he demanded.

"Hi, Dad," Kellach said. "You sure did wake up in a hurry."

"Look, I've got a lot to do. There's a sleeping sickness sweeping through the town, and I've got to get these people out of here. I want you three to go home immediately."

"Nobody's sick anymore, Dad," Kellach said. "We've solved the problem."

Torin wasn't listening. He had returned to his brisk style of ordering everyone around as easily as Suma had transformed back into a boy.

"All right, everyone, just keep moving," Torin thundered. He pointed at a watcher nearby. "You there, help me restore order here." Torin was about to move away, but Driskoll tugged at his sleeve.

"Not now, son." Torin said.

Suma stepped forward and grabbed Torin's arm with his muscular hands. Kellach and Driskoll looked at each other. Driskoll was actually a little afraid for Suma.

Torin stopped. He turned around and glared at the boy.

"Who are you?" he asked icily.

"My name is Suma, and I think you ought to listen to what your sons have to say."

Torin stared at Suma. "All right," he said, turning to Kellach. "Well?"

Suma loosened his grip, and Driskoll could have sworn he saw Torin touch his arm where Suma had grabbed him.

Kellach took a deep breath and told his father the whole story from the beginning.

Torin listened calmly, his dark eyes flashing. "So let me see if I understand," he said in a low voice. "You disobeyed me by going to the cathedral, you destroyed the blacksmith's shop, and you managed to get everyone in town here in this underground cavern. Is there anything else?"

Driskoll, Kellach, and Moyra hung their heads low. "You've about covered it," Driskoll said.

"No," Suma said. "There's a lot more to it, sir. They saved your town. Driskoll figured out how to control the Inevitable, and he ordered it to destroy the Yuan-ti. Moyra helped discover the meaning of the mark of the Yuan-ti although she was asleep through most of it, and she doesn't even know what a hero she

And Kellach did an ice spell that put the Yuan-ti into hibernation. Your city is safe now. Everyone should be awake now that the magic has been weakened by Kellach's ice. And everyone should be able to sleep normally again. And it's all because of these three—especially Driskoll."

Kellach stepped forward. "Suma's right. Driskoll did a lot, Dad. He was the one who helped me remember the ice spell. I was sleeping and I was still pretty groggy. And if it weren't for him, we'd have never met Suma."

"Well," Torin said. "Sounds like you three have been pretty brave."

"Yes, sir," Suma said. "They were."

"And pretty responsible too." Torin looked at Driskoll. He rubbed his chin.

Driskoll couldn't believe what he was hearing. But he also knew that he had changed a lot today.

"Well," Torin continued. "I think you've clearly shown that you're responsible enough to take care of a pet." He gave Driskoll the faintest hint of a smile. "Even if you did practically ruin my office."

"Really?" Driskoll stared wide-eyed at his father.

"Really," Torin answered, flashing another small smile.

Driskoll looked at Kellach and Moyra. Then he looked at Suma, who was grinning at him.

Driskoll grinned back. "That's okay, Dad," he said. "Maybe I'll take you up on it later."

"All right." Torin shrugged. "But listen, I want you kids home as soon as possible." Then he and Zendric merged into the crowd, leaving the four kids alone.

"Wow, Dris," Kellach said. "I thought you wanted a pet more than anything."

Driskoll smiled wearily. "Today, I've been a snake, I've been chased by wolves, and I ran into a dragon's mouth. I think I've had enough animal experiences to last me for a long time."

The others nodded in agreement.

"And besides," Driskoll added with a huge grin. "I've got three best friends. What more do I need?"

ACKNOWLEDGEMENTS

Many thanks to
Nina Hess, Peter Archer, and Linae Foster

MORE ADVENTURES
FOR THE

FIGURE IN THE FROST

A cold snap hits Curston and a mysterious stranger holds the key to the town's survival. But first he wants something…from Moyra. Will Moyra sacrifice her secret to save the town?

DAGGER OF DOOM

When Kellach discovers a dagger of doom with his own name burned in the blade, it seems certain someone wants him dead. But who?

THE HIDDEN DRAGON

The Knights must find the silver dragon who gave their order its name. Can they make it to the dragon's lair alive?

**Ask for KNIGHTS OF THE SILVER DRAGON books
at your favorite bookstore!**

For ages eight to twelve

For more information visit www.mirrorstonebooks.com

TM

Explore the mysteries of Curston with Kellach, Driskoll and Moyra

The Silver Spell

Kellach and Driskoll's mother, missing for five years, miraculously comes home. Is it a dream come true? Or is it a nightmare?

Key to the Griffon's Lair

Will the Knights unlock the hidden crypt before Curston crumbles?

Curse of the Lost Grove

The Knights spend a night at the Lost Grove Inn. Can they discover the truth behind the inn's curse before it discovers them?

Ask for Knights of the Silver Dragon books at your favorite bookstore!

For ages eight to twelve

For more information visit www.mirrorstonebooks.com

THIS IS WHERE
YOUR STORY BEGINS

Create your own heroes and embark on epic tales
of adventure filled with monsters, magic, trouble,
and treasure with the **Dungeons & Dragons**®
roleplaying game. You'll find everything you need to
get started in the **D&D**® *Basic Game* and can take your game
to the next level with the **D&D** *Player's Handbook*™.

Pick them up at your favorite bookstore.

wizards.com/dnd

THE NEW ADVENTURES

Want to know more about the Dragonlance world?

Want to know how it all began?

A Rumor of Dragons
Volume 1

Night of the Dragons
Volume 2

The Nightmare Lands
Volume 3

To the Gates of Palanthas
Volume 4

Hope's Flame
Volume 5

A Dawn of Dragons
Volume 6

By Margaret Weis & Tracy Hickman

For more information visit www.mirrorstonebooks.com

For ages ten and up.
Gift Sets Available

THE NEW ADVENTURES

THE TRINISTYR TRILOGY

The Trinistyr
Ancient holy relic
Cursed symbol of power
Key to Nearra's future . . . or her destruction

WIZARD'S CURSE

Christina Woods

Imbued with vestiges of Asvoria's power, Nearra is convinced
she can restore her magical heritage. Will Nearra find
the strength to break the wizard's curse?
September 2005

WIZARD'S BETRAYAL

Jeff Sampson

Betrayals come to light. New powers arise. And a startling
revelation threatens to destroy Nearra, once and for all.
January 2006

WIZARD'S RETURN

Dan Willis

Can the companions stand together and fight the final battle
for Nearra and Jirah's future?
May 2006

**Ask for DRAGONLANCE: THE NEW ADVENTURES
books at your favorite bookstore!**

For more information visit www.mirrorstonebooks.com

For ages ten and up.

THE NEW
ADVENTURES

THE ELIDOR TRILOGY
Ree Soesbee

CROWN OF THIEVES

As Elidor struggles to keep the crown out of the hands of
an evil wizard, he finds himself drawn back to the one place
that frightens him the most: his own past.
November 2005

THE CRYSTAL CHALICE

As the Defiler's curse holds Vael's health hostage, Elidor searches for
a way to rescue her without succumbing to the evil wizard's demands.
March 2006

CITY OF FORTUNE

Vael lies frozen between life and death, and Elidor must save her.
The answer lies in a chalice that holds a powerful wish. But danger
awaits those with wishes, for the Defiler still lurks in the shadows.
July 2006

**Ask for DRAGONLANCE: THE NEW ADVENTURES
books at your favorite bookstore!**

For more information visit www.mirrorstonebooks.com

For ages ten and up.